ST YOU WAIT AND SEE

BLACK SWAN BOOK  0  552  99341  7

riginally published in Great Britain
Michael Joseph Ltd.

INTING HISTORY

ichael Joseph edition published 1986
ack Swan edition published 1989

ateful acknowledgement is made for permission to
produce excerpts from the following copyright
aterial:
he White Cliffs of Dover'. Words by Nat Burton. Music
Walter Kent. Copyright © 1941 Shapiro, Bernstein &
., Inc., NY, NY, USA. Copyright renewed. Used by
rmission. Reproduced by permission of B. Feldman &
. Ltd., London WC2H OLD.
Ve're Gonna Hang Out) The Washing on the Siegfried
ne' by Michael Carr and Jimmy Kennedy. Copyright ©
939 Shapiro, Bernstein & Co., Inc., NY, NY, USA.
opyright renewed. Used by permission. Reproduced by
rmission of Peter Maurice Music Co. Ltd., London
/C2H OLD.
magination'. Words by Johnny Burke. Music by Jimmy
an Heusen. Copyright © 1940 by Borne Company &
orsey Bros. Music Inc. Copyright renewed. International
opyright secured. All rights reserved. Used by
rmission. Reproduced by permission of Chappell Music
imited, London

This book is set in 11/12 pt Mallard
by Colset Private Limited, Singapore.

Black Swan Books are published by
Transworld Publishers Ltd., 61–63 Uxbridge
Road, Ealing, London W5 5SA, in Australia
by Transworld Publishers (Australia) Pty.
Ltd., 15–23 Helles Avenue, Moorebank,
NSW 2170, and in New Zealand by
Transworld Publishers (N.Z.) Ltd., Cnr.
Moselle and Waipareira Avenues,
Henderson, Auckland.

Made and printed in Great Britain by
The Guernsey Press Co. Ltd.,
Guernsey, Channel Islands.

# Just You
## and S

## Stan Bar

**BLACK SW**

There'll be bluebirds over
The white cliffs of Dover
Tomorrow,
Just you wait and see.

*Part One*

# One

By about seven in the evening the Palmers' party was in full swing and you could hear the noise of it at the end of the street. It was a quiet street, in a quiet town; Patience had opened a window a crack to relieve the build-up of baking heat from the banked fires in both downstairs rooms; the piano was going to accompany the games, and someone – Doris – had started to laugh above the rest.

Ronald said he was sweating like a pig, and young Granville piped up with 'I've never seen a shining pig, Uncle Ronald,' which made for more laughter. Until Ronald, telling Granville 'Then tha's seen nowt, lad', added that the next time he knew of a sow farrowing he would take Granville to see it, and Doris's Audrey, at seven some months younger than Granville, asked 'What's farrowing?' (with Granville waiting for the reply to a question he would have asked himself had not shyness suddenly taken hold of him), when nobody wanted to talk about it.

'Let's get on wi' t'games.'

'Never mind all that.'

'It's Christmas . . .'

'Filling their young minds . . .'

These family parties on Boxing Day were a calendar mark in all their lives; the only time they came back home together. They noticed then how the children were growing and changing, remembered how they first came, like Thomas's Brian now, and how they grew into long trousers and went out to work, like Ronald's James

9

and Arthur. And having done that they looked at and took fresh stock of one another.

There were twenty-two in the cottage when the table had been laid (Ada and Cyril would make them the round two dozen); two more than last year. For Brian was new on the scene and James ('Ask your gran'ma yourself.' 'No, you ask her, Mam.') had brought a young woman. Phyllis was the first of her kind, prompting Sugden Palmer to reflect on what the future might hold: 'They're multiplying like the Tribes of Israel, Patience lass. There's bairns still to come – who's to say our Doris and our Thomas's wife have done? And our Ella's not even wed yet – and if t'older ones start bringing their chaps and their young women, we s'll be sitting down eating till midnight. Aye, and pawning all we own to pay for it.'

Patience smiled. 'Nay, Sugden, we shall enjoy a few more Christmases, if the Lord spares us; but he won't spare us all that many.'

As it was, they managed with two sittings – children first, with such mothers as were needed to see to the littlest – at the two tables pushed together and nearly filling the living-kitchen. 'Come on, James lad,' said Wilson's wife Florrie as her nephew hung back. 'Sit yerself down and get tucked in.'

'Happen he thinks he ought to be promoted to t'second sitting now he's brought his young woman with him.' This from Doris as she tied a bib on her youngest, Neville, who, at four, was still a messy eater.

'Well, he'll have to have a word with his gran'ma afore next year's do. We s'll have all on to fit everybody in as it is, 'specially if Ada and Cyril walk in.' And James's young woman, a fresh-complexioned girl who had uttered no more than two words since entering the house, blushed furiously and allowed herself to be shown to a place and offered the first cup of tea by Ella, who was near enough to Phyllis in age to know just how she was feeling, and wasn't, unlike some of the others, inclined to make good-natured fun of it.

Ella and her mother had baked in the week before

Christmas (the cake had been made since the beginning of October), but despite years of catering for a big family Patience always at this moment, just before the first onslaught, wondered if there would be enough for everyone. 'I can always open a tin,' was the silent reassurance as she surveyed the laden table.

There was boiled ham, cold chicken, tongue, and stand pies; tomatoes, lettuce, cucumber and vases of celery; pickled onions, chutney and piccallili; and heaped plates of buttered teacake. To follow came red jelly and yellow, trifle, prunes with evaporated milk; tinned pears; jam tarts and lemon tarts, mince pies, and Christmas cake with or without cheese.

'It's all there,' Patience said. 'T'only thing you can't see is t'jam pot.'

'Our Granville won't touch jelly since he was in hospital to have his appendix out,' Florrie was saying. It was nearly eighteen months since Granville had had his appendix removed and Florrie had told them about his aversion to jelly at last year's party. 'They put him on a diet straight after his operation. Everybody else was having hot dinners but all they brought him was jelly. Two colours, mind, but he said it had all ice on it. Fair put him off. There isn't a spoonful of jelly crossed his lips since.'

'Aren't you going to try some of your gran'ma's jelly, Granville?' Ella asked. 'You can't go through life not liking jelly, y'know.'

The men had gone into the front room out of the way until the bairns had been fed. They sat in a semi-circle round the huge fire and talked about work: Sugden, his three surviving sons, Ronald, Wilson and Thomas, and his son-in-law, Doris's husband, Jack Walford. Sugden was retired; the others, except Jack, who worked in railway-wagon repairs, were colliers as he had been. All of them, at present, were in regular work. All of them remembered vividly the beating the miners had taken in 1926, and the decade since then had given them no confidence in the permanence of jobs. They thought themselves lucky in living where no one industry dominated, so that depression hit piecemeal. But while deprivation was never total, a general reassuring prosperity was something that kept its distance too. It was a small town, of stone, with a raw pink fringe of council houses, its steep streets surmounted by the spire of a church on a hill above a wide river valley. A town of ruggedly independent chapels as well, and small shop-keepers; of people who, within the limits of their dependence, were independent also, respectful without servility towards the well-to-do – for the most part recognisable as their own kind in better circumstances, the high walls which contained their houses and lawns flanked by lanes where workers' cottages stood. In the early hours the still dark streets would ring with the clog-irons of the colliers walking to the nearest pit, across the river; followed later by the laughter-interrupted murmur of mill girls off, in turn, to their shift. At certain times of the year, when the women's walk coincided with dawn, they would exchange greetings with the one-armed lamplighter who strode the empty streets, lifting a long pole to douse the light of gaslamps whose mantles he would return to and touch into a soft glow at dusk.

Ada and Cyril arrived when the grown-ups were at table and the young ones sent into the front room now vacated by the men. James had said he thought that he and Phyllis would go for a walk and his mother asked where they were thinking of walking to in the dark. Just a change of air, James said, and his mother said she hoped he wasn't planning on sloping off now he had had his tea, because the party was not over yet. James's brother Arthur, who at seventeen was poised even more awkwardly between the grown-up world and that of childhood (for one thing, he worked underground with his father and brother but was not yet legally entitled to go into a pub with them for a drink, a circumstance his mother was grateful for but which irked him no end), said he wouldn't mind a walk too; but James said something quietly to him which nobody else could hear and he seemed to change his mind. So with Thomas's wife Winnie, who would have taken charge, upstairs trying to get young Brian to sleep so that she could enjoy the party in peace, Arthur was told off with his sister Mary to keep an eye on the smaller ones and see that none of them fell on to the fire.

Ella got the scent of Ada's toilet water carried on the cold draught she and Cyril brought in with them, which stirred the coloured paper-chains hanging under the low ceiling. She took her sister's fox fur. 'Give her your hat an' all,' Sugden said. 'It's not a funeral.' And Ada relinquished it with a smile whose studied sweetness worked hard to convey the spirit of good will in which she came. Ella, who had often been ruffled by her sister's airs, thought it could not be denied that Ada brought something special into the house: a feeling of other places and other ways.

That they were late was only what most there had expected. (Some, if asked, would have said they felt honoured that they had come at all. They had all of thirty miles to travel and only their master's motor car to do it in; their employers had gone to spend the holiday in Bournemouth, leaving Ada and Cyril with the responsibility of keeping the house warm, the plumbing unfrozen and the indoor plants watered. Sarcasm was given regular exercise in the Palmer family.) Still, here they were and it was Christmas, a time to forget all those little resentments and hope there was no one who would find it too hard to bite back the kind of remark that would get Ada going.

Room was made for them at the table, food passed and more hot water added to the tea-pot. Sipping from the cup given her, Ada wrinkled her nose and said, 'Ella, I don't want to be a nuisance but would you mind if Cyril and I had a fresh pot of tea? This is a bit stewed.' And Ella reached a smaller pot from the cupboard over the sink as Patience said, 'It was fresh made for us to sit down.'

'Perhaps so, Mother,' Ada said, 'but you've already had the best out of it. One and a half spoons, Ella, no more,' she called to her sister. 'If I'd thought I could have brought some broadleaf with me; it's what we always drink at home.'

'You're at home *now*, Ada,' Sugden said, 'and you can enjoy what everybody else is having.'

'I know, Father, and I've already said I don't want to make a fuss; but you might remember that some of us get out of the habit of collier tea.'

'While you're here, Ada,' Sugden said, 'you can make do with what your mother provides and I pay for.'

Ella, surprised at where the friction was coming from, and how early, couldn't think what had got her father's back up, but realised that the moment anybody else joined in a full scale row might ensue; so she said quickly: 'I don't know that we have to have an inquest over a fresh pot of tea. It's nowt to make a song and dance about.' Which appeared to be the wrong thing, for Sugden brought four fingers of one hand flat down on the edge of the table and asked, 'Am I still the master in this house, or am I not?' No one spoke. 'Well then, Ella, don't argue with me, just sit yourself down while there's still summat left on t'table.'

Cyril glanced up briefly from his full plate. He was tucking in without saying anything, and seemingly quite happy with the cup of tea Ella had given him at first. He was easy enough company, Cyril, when he got warmed through; and when it came to party games showed a streak of healthy vulgarity which quite matched that of his brothers-in-law, and which Ada chose to ignore.

The men lingered at the table smoking while the women cleared away and washed up. None of the women smoked except Winnie and she could never bring herself to light up in her father-in-law's house. Sugden was the only pipe-smoker. He sat quiet, shaving slivers off a length of black twist with the worn but very sharp blade of his pocket knife, while the men's talk reverted yet again to the topic of work.

14

'I had this job offered me in South Yorkshire,' Ronald said. 'Early 1919, when I'd just come back from t'war and fancied a change from round here. T'manager set me on and said he'd find me a house.'

'They're too deep, them pits down there, for them 'at's not used to 'em,' Wilson put it. 'I've known men 'at's gone and come back. They couldn't work in that heat.'

'Well, I'd ha' risked that,' Ronald said. 'Only I had a walk round t'village while I wa' waiting for me train, and summat struck me. There wa' nowt in t'vicinity bar pits and farms. And I thought to meself, if there's ever any trouble here there's no other work to go to.'

'What other work do we know?' Wilson asked.

'There wa' none for t'women to go to either, Wilson, that's what I'm tryin' to get across to thee. I've been glad o' Martha's wages from t'mill on more na one occasion, and I'm not too proud to say so. If t'women can't bring summat into t'house in time of dispute, t'coal owners have got you down afore you start.'

'Whenever have t'coal owners been forced to give what they didn't want to?' Wilson wanted to know.

'Oh, there's been once or twice they've made concessions,' Sugden said.

'Not in owt that mattered,' Wilson insisted. 'In 1926 we went back to worse hours and wages than appertained when we struck.'

'Colliers!' Ada was finally driven to exclaim. 'I've never known anybody like 'em. They work harder out of the pit than they do down it.'

'Don't thee believe it, Ada lass,' Wilson said. 'Tha'd know t'difference if tha went down thi'sen.' The men usually modified the broadness of their speech when talking to their womenfolk, but Ella thought that Wilson sometimes deliberately put it on for Ada's benefit.

The talk drifted to the shortcomings of a deputy whom they all disliked but who was now on nights for a spell and so out of their way. 'I hope it's never a choice between nights and t'sack,' Wilson said, 'because I shan't know what to do for t'best.'

15

'I know what's up wi' thee,' Ronald said.

'I've never hiddied it,' Wilson said. 'It's hearing t'weight come on round three in t'morning. It's summat I never could get used to.'

'What do you mean "the weight come on"?' Cyril asked. He usually showed little interest in pit work, but this had aroused his curiosity.

'I mean when everything 'at's over your head seems to settle,' Wilson said. 'Listen . . .' he raised his hand to the ceiling as a board in the bedroom floor gave under Patience's tread. 'It's like that, only it doesn't spring back; and it's a thousand feet o' rock and soil 'at's letting you know it's there. I've never been one for looking over me shoulder in t'pit, but I could somehow never get used to that.'

'Why does it happen in the middle of the night?' Cyril asked.

'Nay, I don't know.'

'That's when you can hear it,' Ronald said. 'There's nobody getting coal in t'night, so it's quieter.'

'I wouldn't work down there for a pension,' Cyril said.

Ronald said, 'You get used to it, if that's what you're put to. Me father wor a collier. His older brother an' all.'

'My father left t'land to go down,' Sugden said. 'Who knows? If he hadn't done that we might all ha' become gentleman farmers.'

'Well, no lad o' mine's going down,' Wilson vowed.

'Neither our James nor Arthur seemed to know what else they wanted, so there wa' nowt much to be said.' This from Ronald.

'I shall put our George to a trade 'at'll keep him out, if at all possible,' Wilson said. 'And our Granville's got a good headpiece on him, so if we can get him through his scholarship and into t'grammar school he might not have to work with his hands at all.'

'He'll be t'first,' Sugden observed.

'And jolly good luck to him,' Ada exclaimed. 'Somebody's got to be the first, unless they're going to stick in the same rut for ever.'

16

Sugden pulled a face and opened his mouth as though to challenge Ada on her choice of words; but the door opened and James and his young woman came in from their walk. Phyllis's face already showed plenty of colour from the cold air but it deepened as she went through the business of meeting two more of James's relatives and Ada and Cyril had a good look at her.

'Where's your young man, then, Ella?' Cyril turned his head to speak to her as she moved across the room behind him.

'What young man's that?'

'Nay, you tell me. Every time I come I expect to see some lucky young chap with his feet under the table.'

'You're one off, then, aren't you?'

'It seems like it. I don't know why, though. You're not ill-favoured.'

'Our Ella's over-particular,' Doris offered.

'How am I?' Ella protested. Anybody would think they were queueing at the door and she was turning them away.

'What if she is?' Ada said.

'It's not saying much for you, Jack, any road,' Ella said to Doris's husband. 'If our Doris thinks I'm particular it seems to mean she wasn't.'

Florrie said she thought that Ella was still enjoying having the house to herself after spending all her life growing up with the rest of them. And it was true that as the last left at home she had acquired something denied the others, which was her parents' undivided attention.

Ada protested that Ella had always been made much of by all of them. Spoiled, even; since she had been a surprise, coming along when everybody – Patience included – had thought Thomas the last.

Here, though, the conversation turned aside again, that subject being too delicate for open discussion. For when Ronald, in receipt of a letter from Martha, had written to his parents from base camp in France in 1917 to say that he had applied for compassionate leave so that he could marry as soon as possible, Patience was

17

already beginning to show with Ella. Her choice then had been to keep away from the ceremony or, as she did, to go and offer everyone the chance of saying that when a mother past forty could not control herself, what example was that for a son? Yet wasn't there something only too understandable in the instinct which let nature offer its own assuagement of grief? Edward had been lost on the Somme in 1916. And then, after Ella was born, and while Ronald was spared, John, mercifully too young for the war, had died in the influenza epidemic of 1918. So Ella was the treasured youngest, and one of the six surviving of nine.

'What time is it by a good watch?' Ronald asked Sugden. He was holding his own pocket watch to his ear as he nodded at Sugden's heavy cased hunter hanging beside the fireplace. 'It'll be right, won't it?'

'Be summat new if it isn't.' There wasn't a clock in the house; the activities of the Palmer family had been timed by Sugden's watch for as long as any of them could remember. Sugden pulled the watch towards him on its chain and opened the cover. 'What do you want to know t'time for, anyway?'

'Nay, it's this watch o' mine. I can't rely on it any longer.'

'Will it mend?'

'Not at price I paid for it. You buy watches like this and use em till they're done for.'

'There's nowt beats a reight watch.'

'You want summat you're not frightened o' taking down t'pit.'

'I never needed a watch down t'pit,' Sugden said. 'I allus knew what time it wa' within a quarter hour.' He could still, now, without an alarm, be relied on to wake and knock on Ella's door to get her up every working morning.

'There's nowt spoiling, any road, is there?' he asked now, and Ella twigged his little game.

'Not 'at I know of,' Ronald said.

'Well then.' Sugden waited for someone else to speak, then said, 'T'Masons is open, if that's what tha're fretting over.'

'Isn't it allus open at this time?'

'He varies according-ly to his custom. But I've just heard somebody talking in t'yard afore they went in. He'll have t'first two or three pints through t'pipes by now.'

'Well, there's summat given me a rare thirst,' Wilson said. 'I don't know what it was.'

'I thought that stand pie wor a bit on t'salty side,' Thomas said.

'Is there any tea left in t'pot, Ella?' Sugden asked.

'I might squeeze half a cup for you, if you don't mind it a bit stewed.'

The moment she had said the word 'stewed' it occurred to Ella that Ada might think she was being got at, and she glanced quickly in her direction. But both she and Cyril seemed to be absorbed in talking to Martha.

'Nay,' Sugden said, 'it's not for me: it's for these three thirsty lads.'

'I can soon make some more.'

'Or happen t'bairns have left some pop,' Sugden went on.

'You've no need to mak' gam', Father,' Ronald said. 'We all know what you're up to.'

'I'm after keeping you three out o' t'pub,' Sugden admitted. 'Let t'bairns have their enjoyment and when they're off to bed you can have yours.'

'There's nowt to stop us sendin' round wi' a jug,' Thomas suggested.

'Aye, there is. I'm not having you breathing ale all over them young 'uns. We'll let t'day progress like it allus has.'

And with the washing-up done and the second table taken away, so that, as Sugden said, you could once more see the pattern in the carpet – his recurrent joke, because there was no carpet, only a number of mats and rugs on the bare stone floor of the kitchen – the day had progressed as far as the games.

They started with those like Musical Chairs and Pass the Parcel, which got everyone going and gave Ronald's and Martha's Mary a chance to show how much progress she had made with her piano lessons. Then there was Oranges and Lemons; then Winks, which involved the women sitting in a circle, each with a man standing behind her. One of the men had an empty chair in front of him and it was his job to signal one of the women to dash across from her own place by a wink that registered and was acted upon before her keeper could grab her shoulders and hold her back. After this group, when some of the older people were glad of a breather, Ronald and Wilson, sometimes aided and abetted by Cyril, would set up games of a different kind, involving the erection of elaborate makeshift equipment in the front room and the leading in of blindfold children. Wilson was the master of comic invention, always thinking of some new practical joke to render small children near hysterical with laughter. 'That's enough, Wilson. If he laughs any more he'll be sick and he'll surely never sleep tonight.' One which all the older ones knew, called Kissing the Blarney Stone, Wilson set up for James's young woman. James knew what was going to happen but could neither protest nor warn Phyllis for fear of being a bad sport. So he watched, hoping more than anything that she wouldn't take serious offence, while a number of volunteers were led in and put through the ritual and were all sitting round as an audience when Phyllis, blindfold, was brought into the room. There was some preliminary mumbo jumbo and chanting of nonsense rhymes before the blarney stone itself was reached and Phyllis was spun round several times and put down on her knees before it. Then it was that Doris took it into her head to join in – with what reason except mischief that was near to malice Ella couldn't make out – and pushing Ronald aside offered the formed cleft of her own fleshy forearms pressed together for the touch of Phyllis's lips. She was back in her chair before the blindfold was removed and Phyllis was presented with the sight of Wilson hoisting his trousers over what had seemingly a moment ago been his bare behind.

Phyllis's soft cheeks flamed. She didn't know where to look as the younger children rolled on the floor and the grown-ups lay back in their chairs, helpless. 'Her face!' was all that Doris could manage between shrieks. 'Go on, lass, laugh,' Ella found herself willing the girl, until she realised that Phyllis had not yet taken in the truth of the situation, the joke within the joke. James darted across and helped her as, still dizzy from being spun, she tried to get to her feet. As he held her she gave him a little resentful push and he looked quickly round, his own expression half resentful, half embarrassed, to see who was watching.

Ella went into the kitchen, which was empty for the moment. She took a key from its hook and walked down the yard to the w.c. She smelled cigarette smoke as she opened the door. Combined with a still-warm seat it could only mean that Winnie had nipped out for a drag; probably while everybody else was busy watching James's young woman put to the test.

Coming out into the yard again and locking the door behind her, Ella drew closer to her neck the shawl she had thrown over her shoulders and stood breathing the cool dry air as she looked up at the sky. It was a clear night. There were stars to be seen. There would be a frost later. In front of her the Sadlers' house lifted its bulk of blackened stone above the dividing wall. Some of its windows had coloured glass in them, protected by strong, small gauge wire mesh. There was a turret at one corner, and other, smaller windows of various shapes looking out of rooms that Ella could not picture in her mind's eye. There was no light to be seen anywhere in the house. The Sadlers, like Ada's employers, had gone away for Christmas. She wondered if they had been at parties, perhaps in a house even bigger than their own. Ella knew what they were like from the pictures. People stood around drinking. Someone played the piano (a grand, of course, not an upright with brass candle-holders) while someone else sang. In another part of the room other people played bridge. If the house was very big there might be dancing. You could, of course, find the same sort of thing in the posher hotels; but to Ella, spending Christmas in a hotel announced one thing about you. You were lonely and had no family to draw around you. Her own family could be exasperating at times, what with the petty squabbles, the jealousy, the backbiting, the feuds; but these Boxing Day get-togethers were something everybody enjoyed and would miss when they were no longer there. At which thought, Ella fell to musing about how much longer they might survive. Presumably as long as at least one of the parents was alive; though not once they were both gone. But if all went well she would have time to introduce her own children as Thomas and Winnie were introducing theirs. If, that was to say, her life followed the pattern of most other women's she knew and she found a chap in the next two or three years who she was willing to go to the altar with.

The rattle of the sneck drew her head round. A wedge of gaslight fell across the yard for a moment as the house door opened and shut. The person who had come out stood looking down the yard, then walked towards her as his eyes accustomed themselves to the dark. 'Is that you, Ella?' It was James, her nephew.

'What are you doing?'

'Having a breather.'

'You'll catch cold, standing out here after that heat.'

'Is your young woman all right?'

'I'm walking her home in a minute.'

'Did your Uncle Wilson upset her?'

'You know how it is when you're among a lot of strangers: you're soon embarrassed.'

'As long as it hasn't put her off us altogether.' James didn't answer. 'Is it serious?'

'I expect she'll get over it.'

'She will if she's anything about her. But I didn't mean that. I meant between you and her. On your side.'

'You know as well as I do, Ella, 'at you don't bring a

22

lass home unless it is serious. Once they've seen her they
expect to see her again.'

'She wouldn't call it off over a daft thing like that,
surely?'

'Who said she would?'

'You sounded very doubtful. And I was watching you
both in there.'

'Oh, were you?'

'No need to get ratty with me. I'm your Aunty Ella,
remember.'

'Aye, well, all t'same, I'm beginning to wish I'd never
brought her.'

'Better for her to know the worst to begin with, James.
You can't keep her away from your family for ever. She
might get to thinking she's too good for us.'

'Not you, Ella. You know I'd never think a thing like
that about you.'

'We're not talking about you.'

'Well, Phyllis, then. It's just me dad when he gets that
side out, and me Uncle Wilson and Auntie Doris.'

'They're not who she'll have to live with.'

'Ey, not so sharp, our Ella. You're galloping on a bit,
aren't you?'

'You said you'd not have brought her home if it hadn't
been serious, so that must be what you have in mind. Just
as long as you don't get somebody who spends all her
time trying to make you into summat you're not, is all I
want to say.' James scraped the dust of the yard with the
toe of his shoe. 'Not that there isn't plenty of room for
improvement.'

He wasn't laughing. 'I don't think I'm the answer to a
maiden's prayer.'

'I don't see why not, providing it's the right maiden.
Does she come from t'better sort?'

'Her father has an insurance round.'

Which, Ella thought, was quite enough to let her think
she was Somebody and her family be not at all keen on
seeing her getting hooked to a collier. But it was not her
place to speak aloud a thought like that. She had stuck

her nose in quite far enough. And uninvited, what's more.

'Well I shan't chase her if she wants to act silly buggers,' James said with sudden defiance.

'No,' Ella said, 'but there's no need to get stroppy before she gives you a good cause.'

'No.'

Ella shivered. 'Do you want the lav key?'

'Aye. Ta. I'd better not keep her waiting till she's forced to come down here.'

'Why not?'

'Because I think she'll either do herself an injury or wet herself before she does. She never goes at our house, y'know. Me mam only noticed last week. They've got a lav inside, y'know, and a bathroom, with rugs on t'floor and a little mat on t'lav seat. All pink.'

'A mat on the lav seat?'

'Well, a sort of cover to match the rugs.'

'Flippin' heck.'

'That's what I thought when I saw it.'

'You've been, then?'

'Oh, aye. They're not bad, her mam 'n dad. She's got a younger sister who's a bit of a . . .' He sighed. 'Don't you ever have any trouble like this, Ella?'

'Not so far, no.'

'It's a pity,' James said, ' 'at they don't let aunties and nephews wed.'

'Don't they?' Ella asked.

'I don't think so. I could always find out. Me mam'll know. She's well up in all that sort of thing.'

'If they did you and me could get together, do you mean?' Ella said.

'Aye. Wouldn't it save a lot o' bother?'

'In one way, happen so,' Ella said. 'But what makes you think I'd be willing to marry into a family like ours?'

James guffawed. He was still laughing as he opened the lavatory door and Ella was walking up the yard.

# Two

This had been the year they took over Mary Ellen Matlock's twice-yearly lodger. Mary Ellen recommended them to Mr Keighley when her husband died and she decided to go and live with her daughter. Mr Keighley travelled in clocks and watches for a firm of Birmingham wholesalers. He needed accommodation for five days in spring and five in autumn while he visited his customers in the West Riding towns, and though Ella was sure he was used to better things, he seemed not to mind their lack of an indoor lavatory and running hot water, his quiet, abstemious nature being well satisfied with the cheap and simple, but clean and wholesome fare provided for him.

Some four or five weeks before each visit a letter would arrive from Mr Keighley, hoping it found them as it left him, confirming the date of his arrival and trusting the arrangement was still convenient. It was Ella who replied. Patience could only just write her name – though she could read enough to shop and make her way about – and while Sugden could write a simple message it was a labour he was always willing to be relieved of. On the day, Mr Keighley would arrive by train, walking up from the station to knock at the door and wait for admission on his first appearance, with him his well-worn case of samples and a valise containing his personal effects. He and Mrs Keighley were a childless couple, and during the first hour or so he would enquire about the members of the Palmer family whom he knew and listen with polite interest to news of those he had not happened to meet.

He was, as Patience often said, not a minute's bother. Out directly after breakfast and not seen again till high tea, his wants were confined to those two meals, a clean, comfortable bed, and a large jug of hot water in his room, morning and evening. On light nights he would take little strolls about the neighbourhood, calling perhaps to see people whose acquaintance he had made over the years, and sometimes he liked to stand and talk to Sugden by the hen run or down the vegetable garden. Sugden cultivated a good garden, and Mr Keighley was always interested in expert knowledge, from wherever it came and with whatever subject it was concerned. When the nights were drawing in he might pay a couple of visits to the local cinema, whose programmes changed three times a week. He rarely drank, except to accept a glass of beer when, as he occasionally did, Sugden sent Ella with a jug to the out-sales window of the Masons Arms.

Being used to permanent employment Mr Keighley bent a sympathetic ear to news of the fortunes of working men, which were at the mercy of economic forces more fickle than those ruling his trade; and when the talk by the fire moved on to larger matters such as the state of the country, Sugden, while not surrendering the validity of his own experience and the rough-hewn philosophy by which he had lived, deferred to the carefully expressed opinions of Mr Keighley, a man who saw much more of the world at large than he did. 'I don't think he can be a Labour man,' Sugden said, 'but he talks fair for all that.' Ella liked to see them together like that: the simple, sometimes awkward courtesy of the raw-boned ex-miner contrasting with the gently put but obviously well thought-out views of the small, neat, rather plump salesman. Both had grey hair, and spade-shaped moustaches which partly shielded their mouths. There was yellow in the roots of Mr Keighley's, which, since he didn't smoke, Ella took to indicate that he had once been fairhaired. He must have been younger than her father, but they always seemed to her of an age, both of them

26

endowed with an equal weight of authority drawn from the patterns of their dissimilar lives.

Ella looked forward to Mr Keighley's visits. She would not otherwise have come into such close contact with a man of his kind. He was not a lively man and he rarely laughed out loud, but she found his gravity and calm, his meticulous habit, his good manners and his sense of what was right and proper somehow reassuring. How he did things was how they were done in another sphere of life. You felt that people did not raise their voices to one another in that life, that they were not habitually rough and neglectful and harshly sardonic, but gentle, considerate and courteous, and that living itself must be more deeply rewarding as a consequence. She was not uncomfortably out of place at the mill; she could handle two looms and she mixed easily enough with the other women. But though they were generous enough with help in time of trouble, she found their sharpness of tongue, their aptitude for squabbling and their jeering reaction to expressions of finer feelings wearing. Their marriages, like those of her brothers and sisters, seemed to her like contests of will, in which lines had been drawn and positions adopted for prolonged and unyielding defence. They lived as though you dared never let your guard down or you would be put upon for ever. Ella wanted none of it. She felt that there must be something better, and if she could not find it she would do without altogether.

On an August day in 1938 there arrived in the post an envelope bearing Mr Keighley's sloping and rather ornate handwriting. They had been expecting word from him, but when the letter was passed for Ella to read to her father and mother she found that Mr Keighley would not this time be coming alone. He did not, he said, wish to impose on their kindness, but could they just this once find room for both him and a colleague. They must not go to any special trouble, the fare they provided for him would be quite satisfactory, but he realised that it might not be possible and if so would they be kind enough to try to find similar accommodation for Mr Strickland nearby. There was a second bed in Ella's room, left over from the crowded years when she and her brothers and sisters had slept three to a room – even, when they were small, head to toe, three to a bed. They could either move that or Ella herself could swap for a few days, providing the two men did not mind sharing. Ella wrote to that effect and received a reply almost by return of post, saying that the arrangement was quite acceptable.

Ella never could recall afterwards what mental image of Mr Keighley's colleague she had conjured up in advance of his coming, because it was wiped out the instant she answered the knock on the door and saw, standing quite five or six inches taller than his companion, a lean young man of no more than twenty-five or twenty-six, with brilliant blue eyes and long fair eyelashes, and a head of thick wavy blond hair which was revealed when he took off his hat on crossing the threshold, and seemed in perpetual danger of brushing the low, whitewashed ceiling. Doris had chanced to call with Neville and suddenly – as Sugden came in from the garden, having seen the two men cross the street – the room felt overcrowded in a way it never did when they were all together at Christmas; for members of a family move easily among one another, and politeness does not prohibit touching.

'Well now, Mr Keighley,' Sugden said. 'Here we are again. Did you have a good journey?'

'No trouble, Mr Palmer.' He shook hands with Sugden and introduced his colleague. 'This is Mr Strickland. Mr and Mrs Palmer, their daughter Ella – Miss Palmer – and another daughter, Mrs, er, Walford. Isn't it?'

'That's right. Pleased to meet you.' A gratified smile had come to Doris's face as her married name was recalled.

'Come you upstairs,' Patience said, 'and I'll show you where you are. We're not allus as throng as Briggate,

28

Mr Strickland, and I'll have you something to eat on the table in half an hour.'

Mr Strickland's nostrils were dilating at the odours coming from the fireplace oven. 'It smells splendid.'

'It's a nice bit of stew, and I'll soon have you some dumplings to go with it. We don't go in for fancy trimmings here, Mr Strickland, so you'll soon learn to make yourself at home. Bring that kettle of hot water off the hob, Ella,' she added as she opened the door to the stairs, 'and follow us up with it. They'll happen feel better for a wash and a tidy.'

'They're a couple of sobersides, aren't they?' Doris said, when Patience and Ella had come down again. 'More like undertakers' men.' She owned a voice that carried, and Patience stepped back and shut the stairs door properly.

'They're not cheapjacks standing a market,' she said. 'They've a position to keep up.' Her daughter's remark had irritated her. 'For heaven's sake wipe that bairn his nose.'

Across Neville's grubby top lip were two pale snot trails, one of which was channelling a fresh green thread.

'Wipe it!' Doris took out a balled handkerchief and darted it roughly at the boy's face. 'I do nowt but wipe it from morn till night. He's never free o' cold.'

'Then you want to get some nourishment into him and grease his chest with vapour-rub of a night.'

'Nay, Mother, he's that faddy he nobbut eats enough to keep a sparrow alive; and you can't force it down him. He allus was a sickly 'un. There's been times when I thought we wouldn't rear him.'

This last remark Ella thought astoundingly tactless, uttered, as it was, in front of the lad himself. But he just stirred, fretful, between his mother's knees and asked plaintively, 'Aren't we goin' home yet, Mam?'

'Aye, we'd best be off, or our Audrey 'ull be locked out.'

They left, Neville clutching a penny which Patience

had given him, with the admonishment to Doris: 'And don't let him spend it on spice to spoil his tea.'

'It's no good givin' him money an' then telling him he can't spend it, Mother.'

'Learn him to save money without it burning a hole in his pocket, can't you?' Patience said.

She and Ella were left alone. Sugden had already returned to his garden. His daughter Doris exasperated him and he preferred to keep out of her way. Patience sighed as she rolled and floured dumplings on the baking-board.

'There's nowt wrong wi' that lad's appetite 'at a bit o' tempting wouldn't cure. He's eaten well enough here, at his grandmother's table. It's our Doris: she doesn't seem to have t'gumption she wa' born with.'

Ella's father and Mr Keighley sat in the early evening and talked about the likelihood of war. It was inconceivable, Mr Chamberlain had said, that we should be drawn into another war with Germany over a faraway country that we knew little about. That was Czechoslovakia, whose name, though she didn't think she could spell it, Ella could pronounce because she had heard it so many times on the wireless. Inconceivable or not, gas masks had lately been issued and people were digging holes in their gardens for air-raid shelters.

So we had sacrificed the Czechs in the hope of peace, Mr Keighley said, but where, he asked, would Hitler's eye fall next?

'You don't reckon he'll be satisfied, then?'

'Not him. Particularly as we've probably convinced him that we won't fight whatever he asks for.'

'Nay,' Sugden Palmer said sombrely, 'it seems only two minutes since t'last time.'

'Twenty years,' Mr Keighley said, 'and already Europe's at the brink again. You'd be too old for the last one, Mr Palmer?'

'Aye, and I'm damn' sure I'll be too old for t'next. All t'same, I had two sons in that – one 'at never came back – and I've one, if not two, 'at's right age for this – not to mention a couple o' grandbairns.' He sighed. 'It sometimes seems to me 'at all your life is one long trouble. A world war and t'best part of a generation wiped out. No work for them what's left, and now it starts all over again.'

'Well, *if* there is another war,' Mr Keighley said, '– and God forbid that it should come to it – I don't think we shall see the wholesale slaughter we knew before, when thousands were killed in a morning, trying to capture a few hundred yards of ground.'

'You don't think so?'

'No. It won't be trenches this time. It will be tanks and aeroplanes.' Mr Keighley allowed himself a thin little smile. 'So perhaps you'd be advised to dig up some of that fine garden of yours and put in a shelter.'

'Nay, I've a good deep keeping-cellar 'at'll manage us better than a few sheets o' corrugated iron. And I don't know 'at there's a lot round here worth their bother. It's places like yours,' Sugden pointed the stem of his pipe at Mr Keighley. 'It's them places they'll be after.'

'I'm only too afraid you're right.'

'D'you think we can change t'subject for ten minutes?' Ella's mother said. 'I'm getting fair mithered with all this war talk.'

'Turning your back on it won't stop it happening,' Sugden said.

'And neither will talkin' about it from morn till night,' Patience gave back. 'Begging your pardon, Mr Keighley. You know we allus like to hear your opinion about things.'

'Oh, I agree, Mrs Palmer,' Mr Keighley said. 'They'll do what they like whatever *we* say.'

So there was a silence, which Patience eventually broke by saying, 'Your Mr Strickland seems a pleasant young man. Has he been with you long?'

'Getting on for two years. Mostly in the shop, so far. But now he's going to travel on the wholesale side. In fact, we've both got promotion. Mr Strickland's coming out and I'm going back in.'

'You mean to say we shan't be having the pleasure of your company any more?'

'It's good of you to express it so nicely, Mrs Palmer. But I've been at it for a good many years, and it really is a job for a younger man. I didn't intend to leave without telling you. And if Mr Strickland coming here is going to be a bother, well, there's absolutely no obligation on your part.'

'We shall have to see what he thinks himself. A younger man might want summat a bit fancier than we can offer.'

'Then he's someone who doesn't know when he's well off,' Mr Keighley said, and Ella's mother's face softened with gratification.

Ella, who had been sitting at the back of the room near the window with some darning since getting washed and changed, left the house then. She was going to the pictures to see *The Prisoner of Zenda*. There was just the one show, at half-past seven, and it was only just turned seven when she went out to make the ten-minute walk; but people were talking about the film and she had an idea there might be a queue.

And so there was, but it soon filed in and there were still one or two empty seats when the lights went down and the attendant quietened the young ones on the hard seats at the front, downstairs, during the advertisements. They were noisy again during the first of the shorts, which was about basketmaking, and rowdy in a different way when the next one came on, a comedy, with the Three Stooges. They loved that, but Ella didn't care for it. The Three Stooges were so silly, always hitting one another. Ella preferred Harold Lloyd or Laurel and Hardy, or even Edgar Kennedy, who got himself into some really daft scrapes but was somehow likeable, the way he always came off worst. Then they had to sit through the newsreel, which was days'-old stuff showing Mr Chamberlain and the top men from other countries signing papers which gave part of Czechoslovakia to the Germans, who, every time you saw them, were marching, either with flaming torches, on their way to hear Hitler rant and rave, or with guns into somebody else's country. Always marching. While the commentator talked about the war clouds dispersing once again. At one point, for no reason she could have explained, Ella felt herself go hot then cold. She had not been brought up to admire Neville Chamberlain or Stanley Baldwin or Winston Churchill – Sugden Palmer had been a Ramsay MacDonald man until MacDonald had let down the Labour Party by forming a National Government – but surely they were clever enough to sort it out. Surely the English Channel and the Royal Navy would be enough to ensure that we never saw German soldiers marching through our streets.

It was a curious moment, during which she felt she had peered into the abyss, and she was to remember it all her life. But it was forgotten quickly now as the big picture started and she dipped into the bag of toffees she had bought at the shop on the corner. And oh! she did enjoy the film. It was so romantic and had such lovely people in it: not only Ronald Colman and Madeleine Carroll, but Douglas Fairbanks Junior and Raymond Massey, and dear old C. Aubrey Smith and that Patric Knowles who was too handsome to be real; and her head when it was over was full of a dream of impossible love, so that walking along the street afterwards she didn't straight away register the voice that addressed her from behind. It was a man's voice, deep and resonant, which spoke her name again.

'Miss Palmer.'

Nobody called her Miss Palmer. As she paused in her step, Mr Strickland came up beside her.

'Are you going straight home?'

'Oh. Yes. Sorry. I was miles away.'

'In never-never land?'

'What? Oh, yes. I suppose it was. Have you been to the pictures as well?'

'Yes. I saw you when I came in.'

'Were you on your own?'

'Yes. I don't know anybody here.'

'You ought to have come and sat with me.'

'I didn't want to impose.'

He was adjusting his long stride to hers. All the same, she had to step out briskly to keep up.

'Did you enjoy it?' she asked.

'Oh, yes. I thought it was first class.'

What a funny thing to say about a film. She could not place his accent. It wasn't strong and it seemed a mixture of north and south. Perhaps that was how they spoke in Birmingham, though she suspected that not everybody would have that gentlemanly way with words. 'First class.'

'It's a comfortable little cinema.'

'Oh, yes. Cosy. A bit noisy sometimes, with the kids.'

'And you get some fine films.'

'Oh, not every week.' She laughed. 'Sometimes it's real tripe.'

'But this week: Ronald Colman followed by Robert Donat and Marlene Dietrich.'

'Yes. I liked the trailer for that.'

'Might you be going to see it?'

'If I can manage it.'

'If it was before Saturday, it would be nice to go together.'

Well, she thought, he might not have wanted to impose but he wasn't wasting any more time. Though she must not read too much into a friendly gesture from somebody who was, after all, living in her home.

'We could go either Thursday or Friday,' he was saying.

'Let's see how my jobs work out.'

'You help your mother a good deal, don't you?'

'I like to give her a hand. She's not getting any younger. And having you and Mr Keighley makes extra work.'

'It's very kind of your parents to put themselves about.'

'There won't be two of you for long. I hear we're going to lose Mr Keighley.'

'Yes, he's introducing me to his customers so that I can take over.'

'And you'll perhaps want to make your own arrangements.'

'I haven't really thought about that yet. I feel that I'm still on probation.'

'With us, you mean?'

'Well, yes. I'm a stranger.'

'Mr Keighley was a stranger once.'

'Yes, but he's an older man; more of a generation with your parents. They might not feel as comfortable with a young man.'

'You're not likely to come in roaring drunk, or anything, are you?' Ella said.

'Oh, no, nothing like that.'

'No.' She thought now that she had been a bit blunt, so she explained, 'I've got a couple of brothers who like their beer a bit too much.'

'I'm not teetotal, though,' Mr Strickland said. 'I do enjoy the occasional glass.'

'Oh, me dad's not temperance. But he's seen what too much can do.'

'Wicked things happen when it really gets hold of a man,' Mr Strickland said. 'Or a woman, for that matter.'

'That's even worse,' Ella said. 'A woman 'at drinks is no use to anybody.'

They were nearing home.

'I like this little town,' Mr Strickland said after a silence. 'There's nothing . . . extreme about it.'

There he went again, with those funny expressions of his.

'We had a murder here once,' Ella told him, as if to say he mustn't take things too much for granted.

'Good heavens!'

'A young chap strangled his fancy woman. Well, everybody called her his fancy woman because she was that type, though she wasn't married at the time. He was only eleven pence-ha'penny in the shilling and she drove him till he didn't know what he was doing. But they hung him just the same, poor thing.'

'He won't do it again, then, that's for sure,' Mr Strickland said.

Ella didn't know how to take that.

'There was a lot of feeling about it,' she said. 'But it made no difference. I've always lived here,' she went on in a moment. 'In the same house. I like going shopping to big places, like Leeds and Bradford, but I wouldn't want to live there. All them streets of houses, crammed on top of one another.'

'You should see Birmingham,' Mr Strickland said.

'I can't imagine it.'

Some way from the house, Mr Strickland stopped. Ella turned and looked back at him. How tall and gentlemanly he looked there in the dark, with his white shirt, his neat suit, his hat.

'What's the matter?'

'If you'd rather we didn't go in together . . .'

'What d'you mean?'

'I can walk about for a few minutes if you'd rather go in on your own.'

'Are you bothered they might think things? Is that what you're thinking?'

'It's you I was thinking about. I don't know how you do things in these parts.'

'It won't be inside they'll talk about us. Is that why you didn't come and sit with me in the pictures?'

'Yes.'

She smiled. 'You are funny. But nice with it. We'll give them something to talk about on Friday night, all being well.'

Mr Strickland laughed, showing his teeth in the dark. 'I'll look forward to that.'

A thought struck her. 'You're not married, or anything, are you?'

'No, no.'

'Not that I'm making anything of it.'

'No, no,' he said again. 'I quite understand.'

'We'd better go in, then,' Ella said, 'or they might wonder.'

So that took them quite a way in a short time, Ella thought later. Mr Strickland was right, of course. You thought twice before you were seen out alone with a man, because of what other people would think. And you did not go out with one many times before you were expected to bring him home for inspection. Then you were keeping company: courting. But Mr Strickland was already in the house and Ella could say they were going to the pictures together without anybody making more of it than that.

They went to see *Knight without Armour* on the Friday night. It was all about an Englishman (Robert Donat) who got caught in the Russian Revolution and ended up helping a noblewoman (Marlene Dietrich) to get clear of all those intent on killing her and her like. Ella was so engrossed in the story and the atmosphere of a huge country in turmoil she even forgot who was sitting beside her, and came to with a start once when Mr Strickland stirred to find another place for his long legs and she got a sudden whiff of his toilet soap. On the way home he bought a parcel of fish and chips and some bottled beer to take in as a last-night treat. It was the perfect gesture for him to have made. Patience chuckled as Ella rapidly put plates to warm in the oven, and made jokes about not feeding him enough. Ella, who was not used to drinking, felt her face flush with enjoyment on one glass of light ale, and after the fish and chips, Mr Keighley, who had protested that he wanted nothing but his usual biscuit and hot drink, but who had ended up tucking in as heartily as everybody else, went upstairs and returned with a little flat square box which he held for a moment as he said a few words. Ella always remembered Mr Keighley's hands. She could always see them when she recollected the touching little ceremony: they were white and smooth-skinned, with a dull shine, the fingers tapered. When Mr Keighley held something he often kept the four fingers together as one unit. Ella wondered if it had something to do with his trade as a watchmaker and jeweller. Now he held the little box before handing it to Patience.

'I'd be pleased if you would accept this as a token of my appreciation of your hospitality. I shall always remember with pleasure the warm welcome you've given me and I hope this little gift will help you to remember me.'

'Well . . .' Patience said as she opened the box.

It was a small gilt clock which could stand on its own when you opened its lid.

'Well . . .' Patience said again. Neither she nor Sugden was good at expressing direct thanks.

'Very good of you, Mr Keighley,' Sugden said.

'Can I look, Mother?' Ella said.

'It's a good little movement,' Mr Keighley told them. 'I don't think you'll have any trouble with it. If you do,' he added dryly, 'perhaps Mr Strickland will see to it for you.'

Ella found herself looking at Mr Strickland's hands, to see if there was any similarity with Mr Keighley's. But they were a young man's hands and they moved in an altogether different way. And as she lifted her gaze from them she found Mr Strickland looking at her in a contemplative way. She gave him a quick smile and began to collect the plates and glasses and put them in the sink. She would be out to work the half-shift at the mill before the two men were up in the morning. Immediately after breakfast they would be gone and the house back to normal.

He had said he would write in late February or early March and Ella thought about him in the intervening months with patient pleasure at the thought of seeing him again. He would come again in the spring but in the meantime the dark of winter closed in. It was the time of long evenings and cold early-morning walks down the lane to the mill; of occasional fogs, of big fires and preparations for another Christmas; of the rubs and lotions and mixtures Patience employed to guard Sugden against his tendency to bronchitis and her own to rheumatism in her knees. Ella's niece, Audrey Walford, caught scarlet fever and was confined for weeks in the isolation hospital outside the town. Her nephew, George Palmer, developed a septic growth in his groin after a blistered heel had gone the wrong way. The doctor lanced the growth first at home, then relinquished responsibility to the hospital when further infection set in. Wilson hurt his leg when he got in the road of a runaway tub down the pit, and was brought out to be put to bed at home. Patience trudged from house to house, offering sympathy and what help she could. 'I don't know why if it's got to come it's all got to come at once,' was as far as she went in complaint. A stoicism towards illness was common to all of them and had lingered in Patience's character to this day. She belonged to a generation which knew it to be unusual to raise a full family.

Then, after a rather subdued Christmas, they settled down to live through the worst months till spring.

Ella found herself waiting for the letter. Mr Keighley's had never varied by more than a week or so. Sugden himself remarked on it.

'It'd be about time for Mr Keighley's letter to be arriving, wouldn't, Ella?'

'Any day now.'

'Did yon' young feller say definite he'd be coming?'

'He said we'd be hearing from him.'

'Aye, well then, it's about time.'

Ella did some sewing on Patience's treadle machine: a couple of new frocks, a blouse to go with a skirt she had bought.

But when the letter came it had Mr Keighley's writing on the envelope. Ella was in the open doorway as the postman came and he put it straight into her hand. She held it, puzzled.

'We shan't know what it says till you open it,' Patience pointed out.

Already Ella knew with a sinking heart that something

had gone wrong. Mr Keighley said there had been an unforeseen change in his plans and could he have his old accommodation after all.

'Doesn't he say owt about Mr Strickland?'

'He doesn't mention him.'

'When you write back you'd better ask him if he just wants room for himself.'

Ella did so. Mr Keighley's reply, four days later, confirmed tersely that he would be coming alone.

'Now what's gone wrong there, then?' Patience wondered.

Mr Keighley arrived as he always had, in the late afternoon, walking up from the station with his bags in his hands. The cottage was set down below the street and they saw his legs darken the window before he knocked on the door. It was just as though Mr Strickland had never existed, and his name was not mentioned until they were all at the table for high tea.

'I expect you've been wondering why I'm here and what's happened to Mr Strickland,' Mr Keighley said. They waited. Ella's pulse had quickened. 'I'm afraid he's no longer with the firm.'

'He's left for another job, has he?' Ella asked, when no one else spoke.

'It's a very distasteful business, but you'll have to know.' Mr Keighley pursed his lips. 'The fact is, he was found guilty of dishonesty. Some of the firm's money went into his own pocket.'

'Well!' Patience said.

'He got the sack, then?' Ella said.

'Worse than that, I'm afraid. It was none of my doing, and he had to go, of course; but the firm felt he should be made an example of, so they prosecuted.' Mr Keighley paused, then he said, 'He was sent to prison for three months.'

Ella simply could not take it in.

'You mean that fine-looking young chap turned out to be lightfingered?' Patience said, shaken herself.

Sugden, who had not so far said a word, shifted in his

chair. 'It's happen a good job we'd nowt worth much lying about here.'

'Dad!' Ella exclaimed. 'How can you say such a thing?'

Her father looked at her, frowning. The simplicity of his reaction had shocked her. She did not think it worthy of him. Her colour had risen for all to see.

'A thief's a thief lass,' Sugden said. 'If he'll take one thing he'll take another.'

'I'm sorry now that it fell to me to introduce him into your household,' Mr Keighley said.

'Nay, Mr Keighley,' Patience said, 'he must have taken you all in or you'd never have brought him. I must say, I'd never have thought it meself; but that just goes to show.' She picked up the big pot, offering more tea, and glanced at Ella. 'It's happen as well he's been found out now, before he came here again.'

'I've got to believe it,' Ella was thinking, 'because Mr Keighley wouldn't lie, and he's been found guilty in court. But all the same, I can't. I can't, I can't, I can't.' A dead weight of dismay pressed on her. She felt stifled. She pushed back her chair.

'I'm going out for a while.'

# Three

'Well, make your mind up,' Walter Lindley said, 'are you coming or not?'

Ella was shopping in the butcher's department of the Co-op, where Walter worked. Walter's hair stuck up at the back, though it always looked to have plenty of cream on it. Ella had more than once felt like asking him if he had tried his own beef dripping; especially when he was pestering her as he was now. 'I don't know if I can,' she said, reluctant to give him the outright no.

'You mean you don't know if you want to,' Walter said. 'You don't know if I'm good enough to go out with.'

He was not lowering his voice and Ella looked over her shoulder, but the woman who had followed her in had gone out again without buying anything and for the moment they were alone.

'I didn't say that.'

'It's what you meant, though.'

'Have it your own way.'

Walter wiped a dewdrop off the end of his nose with the back of his red hand. 'I shan't ask you again,' he said; but Ella knew he would. Walter was single-minded and for some time his mind had been set on her. She cringed as the cleaver splitting her lamb chops thudded on to the block within a whisker of Walter's fingers. She did not want to be the cause of his maiming himself.

'I'll have a quarter of potted meat as well,' she said as he took the chops to the scales.

'I don't know what you've got to be stuck up about,' Walter said. 'Anybody 'ud think your father wor a

42

millowner, 'stead of a retired collier.'

Typical of him to discount her emotions and blame her resistance on snobbery. And she did not, in fact, dislike him. It was just that he had been around for as long as she could remember and he did not excite her. She rarely gave him a thought when he was not in front of her face. To be told that Walter had been caught stealing would have shocked her, but not left her with the paralyzing dismay she'd felt on hearing about Mr Strickland.

Walter was asking her to go with him to the summer feast in Gaskell Field, that was all. But if she went and let him spend his money on her, he would, being Walter, begin to take things for granted; as indeed other people would who saw them together. Ella liked the feast. She liked to go with a friend, or preferably two or three; but most of her friends were either courting steady or married, one or two of them already mothers. She was beginning to feel out of things.

She had paid and could have walked out; but she lingered.

'Them eggs is fresh today,' Walter said.

'What do I want with your eggs?' she demanded. 'Me dad keeps hens. He has enough eggs over to sell. And he sells them cheaper than that.'

'All right,' Walter said.

'And he gives thirteen to the dozen.'

'Have you made your mind up, then?' Walter said.

'Yes. I don't want anything else.'

'I mean are you coming to the feast?'

'You're a pest, Walter Lindley.'

'Bloody well have to be with a madam like you.'

'There's no need to swear.'

'I'll meet you at the corner of Church Lane and Walker Street at half-past seven.'

'Will you now? That'll depend, won't it?'

The shop door opened. Two women came in. At the same time the branch manager appeared in the doorway of the cold-room, wiping his hands. Walter moved away along the counter.

'I shall wait ten minutes, then go down on me own.'

The summer feast was the big event in the town's year. It came for three days in a procession of huge, brightly painted containers drawn by steam traction engines, rumbling through the streets at a steady, dignified speed to the smells of oil and hot metal and the glow of polished brass, bringing people to their doorsteps and children to the school-yard railings.

'T'feast's here!'

'Did you see it come?'

'Aye, it went past just as we were playin' out.'

'Is there a lot this year?'

'Tons of it. All sorts.'

Even grown-ups felt a small clutch of excitement at the news that it had arrived. Sugden and Patience, at their age, would do no more than take a leisurely stroll to see it set out in the field; but all the other members of the family would be there at some time, the younger ones for as many hours as possible, and Ella was asked when she was going.

'I thought I might have a walk down tonight.'

'Them as wants had better make t'most of it,' Sugden said. 'It might be t'last any of us'll see for a year or two.'

'They're not stopping coming, are they?' Patience asked.

'They will if there's a war.'

'Oh, you and your war.'

'It's not my war,' Sugden said. 'It'll be everybody's war this time round.'

Ella thought she had better tell them what they would find out anyway.

'Walter Lindley's asked me to go with him.'

'Walter Lindley in t'Co-op butcher's?' Patience asked.

'How many Walter Lindleys do you know?' Sugden said.

Patience ignored him. 'He's enough off to be t'manager, that one.'

'Oh, Walter's all right,' Ella said, vaguely surprised that she should find herself defending him.

'I'm not saying owt against him.'

'His father's just t'same,' Sugden said. 'I've known him

since he wor a lad his'sen and I've yet to see him stuck fast for summat to say.'

'I seem to remember his mother was a decent little body,' Patience said. 'You could do worse than Walter Lindley.'

'Mother, he's only asked me to go to t'feast with him.'

'And I'm only telling you you could do worse.'

'I didn't even tell him I'd go. Not definitely.'

'Don't dangle chaps on a string, Ella. I cannot abide lasses 'at don't know their own mind. Either say you'll go or you won't, but don't have him danglin'.'

Ella sighed. She could not know then, and would not have believed it if told, that she would live to see an age when girls – younger girls than she was now – would go out with whom they pleased, would live with men out of wedlock, and even, in some cases, share a bed with them under their parents' roof.

She heard the fair long before she saw it. She was aware as soon as she stepped out of the house of a distant throb of sound in which, as she drew nearer, it was possible to make out the steam organ of those huge swing-boats, Shamrock and Columbia, from the confused raucous din of amplified music broadcast at full blast. People sauntering down for the evening met the counter-flow of those taking home tired children with toys and cheap coloured novelties clutched in their fists.

'Away early, Jim.'

'Have to be. T'bairns are asleep on their feet an' I've spent up.'

'A good do, is it, this time?'

'It is if you've a deep enough pocket.'

Walter was leaning on one of the iron posts at the end of Church Lane, making people walk round him. He wore well-pressed grey flannels and a white shirt open over the collar of his tweed jacket. He had made an extra special effort with his hair and for the moment it was all stuck down in place. His head was down in his shoulders and he pulled moodily on the last of his cigarette before flicking away the end. Ella thought from the look of him that he had probably given her up, and he didn't see her till something made him look round the second before she spoke.

'Hullo.'

He straightened up. There was at first no pleasure in his face at the sight of her; just a lingering expression of the thought that, at best, she was leaving it as late as she dared and making him wait every second he had said he would.

'Well then,' he said.

'Well then,' she echoed him.

Now she caught the unguarded light of appreciation in his eyes as he looked her over. She was wearing a lemon-yellow ribbon in her almost black hair, one of her new frocks and a newly washed pair of white cotton gloves.

'You off to the vicar's garden party?' he asked.

'You want a slut, Walter Lindley, you go find one. There'll be plenty about tonight.'

'Don't be so touchy. I was only saying you looked smart.'

'Funny way of saying it.'

But she knew his way and was not offended; though something in her yearned for more elegant compliments.

They set off towards the fairground, Walter walking carelessly in the road and leaving the pavement edge for her, where it was impossible to walk abreast.

'By, but there's some fowk about,' Walter said.

'They're perhaps making the best of it.'

'Eh?'

'If there's a war we shall see the last of feasts for a while.'

'Oh, a war. We shall see the last of a lot of things for a long while, if there's a war.'

'Do you think you'd have to go for a soldier?'

'Unless they find summat wrong wi' me 'at I don't know about,' Walter said. 'But let's forget about all that for tonight and have a good time.'

46

As they turned a corner the blast of noise increased. Lights were blazing, though it would not be dark for two hours or more. To the noise and the lights were added the smells of the fair as they entered the field. The scent of trodden grass was often overpowered by the odours of hot toffee and brandy snap, of donkeys and donkey dung, of hot oil and metal and that curious pungent oily electric smell of the dodgem cars as their power-poles sparked and flashed against the overhead grid.

'Now listen, Ella,' Walter said as they passed through the perimeter of caravans and stalls and paused on the edge of the moving crowd, 'stick close by me and if we do get split up come back and wait by this fortune-teller's tent, here. All right?'

'An' if you're a long time I might go in an' have me fortune told.'

'I could tell your fortune for you, if you'd let me,' Walter said.

Ella wondered if Mr Strickland had liked fairs. Whether he did or not, he couldn't be livelier company at one than Walter was. Walter threw himself into it; he liked to have a go at everything. Ella held his coat while he hurled wooden balls at coconuts with increasing ferocity, his colour mounting in his neck and face till she wondered if he might not bring on a stroke, before he gave up and turned away in disgust, saying loudly enough for the stall-owner to hear, 'See how many times I hit that big 'un? It's wedged in. Take a howitzer to shift it. Come on, let's try this shooting-gallery.' He was really rather good at that, once he had got the hang of the rifle he was using.

'You have a go.'

'I can't shoot,' Ella protested.

' 'Course you can. There's nowt to it. I'll show you.' He put money on the counter and received half a dozen fuzzy-flighted darts. He put one into the air-rifle he had been using and snapped the gun shut. It was only an excuse to touch her, she thought, as he reached round her from behind to bring the rifle up and into her shoulder. 'Relax,' he told her. 'Get your back sight and your front sight into line, then squeeze the trigger.' She could smell the soap he had used and his hair-cream and feel the warmth of his breath on her cheek. She twisted her shoulders.

'All right, let me breathe.'

He freed her, stepping back. She fired.

'Ey!' Walter said. 'We could make a crack shot of you.'

'Have I won anything, then?' she asked when she had fired all her darts.

Walter laughed. 'No. They're not givin' stuff away. I've enough for a prize, though. What d'you fancy?' He waved his hand at the goods along the front of the stall. 'D'you want me to carry on an' get enough for one of them big dolls?'

'I've grown out of dolls.'

'What about this, then?' He picked up a box containing a glass dressing-table set. He pushed it into her hands. 'Go on. Put it in your bottom drawer.'

'Well, you've paid for it,' Ella said.

'What? Oh, aye. You get nowt for nowt here.'

Ella did not want to be burdened so early in the evening with something which was in any case hardly worth carrying home. But neither did she wish to hurt Walter's feelings. So she tucked the box under her arm and let him lead her deeper into the fair. At another stall he gave her pennies to roll. A swarthy man in a grease-stained soft hat walked round and round inside the stall like a caged animal, giving change, scooping in the lost pennies and occasionally throwing a few back, like someone dealing from a pack of cards. When one of Ella's coins settled on a space marked one shilling, she waited till she was paid out, then turned away, happy to be a few pence to the good.

They tried the rides. Ella did not mind the Dodgems or the Jungle Speedway. She could even manage the Whip. But she drew the line at the big swings. They watched as the great boats reared vertically, hung there for a

48

second, then plunged again. They sounded to be full of screaming girls. Ella remembered being taken on this by Wilson when she was little. She had clung on in terror during the ride and been sick as soon as her feet touched the ground. Now the boats came to a halt. It was two girls who had been making all the noise. They giggled helplessly now as they staggered and held on to their men.

'No, Walter,' Ella said, as he put it to her again. 'I don't mind going round and round, but not up and down.'

They went into the Wall of Death and watched two motorcyclists defy gravity as they roared round the inside of the big wooden cylinder. There was a line painted round a few feet from the top, to warn the riders.

'Did you hear about that bloke at a feast in Doncaster who came right over the top?' Walter asked. Ella hadn't, but she instinctively lowered her head as one of the bikes swung up directly below her.

'Did anybody watching get hurt?'

'No, they ducked an' he went straight over 'em an' out through the canvas.'

'But what about the people outside?'

'As luck would have it he went out the other way and bounced off the roof of a caravan and ended up in the open field. Broke his back, both his legs and one of his arms. I heard they get paid twenty quid a week.'

'I wouldn't do it for a hundred,' Ella said.

'Oh, I would for a hundred,' Walter said; 'but not for twenty. With that kind o' money I could retire after a few year, mebbe buy me own shop, then get somebody in to run it and sit back in comfort. It's the bloke what runs this 'at makes all the money. He's not risking his neck, either.'

'Would you like to have your own shop one day?'

' 'Course I would. But I haven't a cat in hell's chance on Co-op wages.'

'At least you've got a job, where thousands haven't.'

'Oh, aye, an' if I play me cards right I shall be manager

one day. You don't need to worry about me, Ella. I shall always make out.'

'I'm not worried,' Ella said. 'I was just asking. Not that it's any of my business.'

'You can always make it your business,' Walter said, with a suddenly bashful sideways look at her.

She pretended she had not heard him.

The trouble with fairs, Ella thought as they went outside again, was that nothing lasted for long. You were in, you were out; you were on, you were off. It was pay again every few minutes. You could sit in the best seats at the pictures for ninepence and see two films. For sixpence you could buy a book. Only one with paper covers but a book all the same. Or you could go to the free library and borrow a real book, with stiff backs. Hours of enjoyment there. Here, though, a pound could vanish before you knew it. Not that she was out of pocket, because Walter was paying for everything; which only made it worse, since it meant he was spending twice as much. He did not seem to care. Always into his pocket, always another lot of coins in his hands. She did not think he was going out of his way to impress her; he was naturally openhanded. He didn't like to spoil a good time by worrying about the expense; but if he went on at this rate he would run through a week's wages. Finally, Ella said,

'Walter, don't you think you've spent enough?'

He laughed at her. Her thriftiness pleased him. There were girls who would have let him empty his pockets and then thought it was not enough.

'I save up for it,' he told her. 'I save summat every week. I've a box for me clothes, and another for holidays an' times like this. I'm not a spendthrift, Ella.' He laughed again, boldly, straight into her face. 'T'lass 'at gets me 'ull make a catch.'

'I wonder there isn't a queue,' Ella said.

'It's me what's particular. I don't encourage 'em.'

'Have I to consider meself honoured, then?'

His expression darkened as he scowled, suddenly

50

irritable. 'You can suit yourself.' He stood with his hands shoved into his trousers pockets, his leg swinging as he dented the soft earth with one heel. 'If you're not enjoying yourself don't let me keep you. I can soon find other company.'

Two young men of his own age passed. They eyed him with Ella and called out, 'Nah then, Walter.'

'An' I don't mean them, neither,' Walter said.

Ella blushed. She had meant merely to curb his good opinion of himself, not to upset him. But it seemed you could only go so far. Or she could. Some girls would have enjoyed the power, but she was not sure she wanted the responsibility of it. And now she did not know what to say.

She was saved by the sight of an odd figure coming towards them.

'Look, there's Josh Cutshall.'

Josh wore a crumpled tweed jacket that was too small for him and a shirt without tie which would not fasten at the neck. A vacant good humour shone out of his button-black eyes and a dribble of saliva leaked from one corner of his loose mouth.

As he drew nearer, three young chaps whom Ella did not know came shouldering through the crowd, making people step aside. Josh, who had not seen them, walked directly into their path. One of them bumped him and a second, whom he reeled into, pushed him and sent him sprawling.

Walter ran forward and picked him up. Then he threw back his head and bellowed after the lads,

'Ey, you lot, what yer think yer doin'?'

One of the lads glanced idly over his shoulder, then halted and touched one of his friends.

'What d'you want?'

'I want you, you clumsy buggers.'

They strolled back. They looked, Ella thought, both insolent and dangerous.

'What's up wi' yer?'

'You just walked straight through this poor bugger here. D'you think you own the bloody place, or what?'

'Who wants to know?' the first lad asked, at the same time darting glances past Walter to see who might be with him.

'I bloody do.'

'Is he your brother, or summat?'

'What's that got to do with it?'

'I just thought you looked like brothers,' the lad said. His mates laughed.

One of them said, 'Come on, George. He's not worth the bother.'

'Nay,' George said, 'he's spoilin' for summat.'

'I'm spoilin' to show thee some manners,' Walter said, his colour furious now.

'Don't be daft, lad,' George said, 'there's three of us.'

'Is that how tha fights, then?' Walter asked. 'Well, I'll take thee first an' thi mates after. Or I'll take all three of you at once. I'm not fussy.'

He began to take off his coat.

'No, Walter,' Ella said.

'You just hold this.'

It was as he looked away for a second in handing her the coat that the lad came at him.

'Look out, Walter!'

Walter stepped aside and struck, catching the lad off balance. The blow took him on the side of the head and spun him round. He went down on one knee and put his hand to the ground to save himself. As men passing by realised what was happening they drew their women-folk clear of the scuffle. Some went on, wanting no part of it; others stood to watch. Ella found herself on the edge of a cleared space. Josh had scurried off and as she held Walter's coat she felt herself singled out. Her cheeks flamed as she heard someone ask what the fight was about and the reply came: 'That lass, there, by t'look of it.' Walter stood over George and when he got up hit him again. Ella had not known that Walter could handle himself as well as this, but she still felt frightened and ashamed.

George was not wearing a jacket, just a shirt and a

sleeveless pullover. He was frowning now and going red in the face because he could not get over the setback of having been hit twice by Walter. One of George's mates seemed to think Walter's second blow had not been fair; or he pretended that for an excuse to join in.

'Ey!' he said. 'Let him get up.'

He had taken hold of Walter's shoulder and started to pull him round, but Walter shrugged free, spun round on his own and banged the lad straight in the middle of the face. Then the third lad jumped on Walter, his arms round his neck, and dragged him to the ground. Ella knew that Walter hadn't a chance with all three of them on top of him and she did not wait to see if anybody would help, but in a fit of temper that surprised her with its ferocity, waded in herself, grasping the nearest of the lads by the back of his shirt and hauling on him with all her strength.

'Leave him alone,' she heard herself shouting. 'That's enough. Leave him alone.'

It was all she was aware of, that boiling over of rage at the stupidity of them all, Walter included, before a blow she did not see coming and which she thought afterwards was not deliberate but the unguarded swing of an elbow from a tangle of limbs, slammed her in the bridge of her nose and sent her reeling back, her fall cushioned by someone's quick hands.

She came to on the grass by the canvas wall of one of the sideshows. There was a folded coat under her head and a woman she did not know was dipping the end of a towel into a bucket of cold water and pressing it to her, Ella's, face. She shut her eyes again, then opened them as her nostrils took the smell of beer-breath and a man, leaning back from peering at her, said, 'She's coming round.' It was her eldest brother, Ronald. Someone else held her hands, squeezing and patting.

'Are you all right, Ella?' That was Walter.

Ronald supported her shoulders as she struggled to sit up. There were other people around her, leaning in, peering. They reminded her of people gathered round a dog which had been run over and dragged into a yard until the vet could get there and destroy what was left of it. How it had whined! The sound of it had followed her home and come back that night to haunt the still moments before she fell asleep.

'Tell them to go away,' she said. 'I'm all right.'

Ronald twisted on his hunkers. 'Let her get some air, will yer! There's nowt to see.' He spoke to Walter in a savage undertone. 'By God, lad, tha're a reight 'un to bring a lass out an' let her get knocked about like this.'

'I didn't know she was going to join in.'

'She joined in to save thy skin by t'look of it. What wa' tha doin' takin' three of 'em on?'

'They didn't fight fair.'

'Tha wor a fool to rely on it. Wa' yer fightin' over her? Is that what it wor about?'

'He was stickin' up for Josh Cutshall,' Ella said.

'Oh, wor he? How do you feel now? Can you stand up?'

'It's me nose,' Ella said. 'It feels as big as a football.'

'It looks about same size,' Ronald said. 'Tha're a bonny picture to tak' home.'

Ella glanced down at herself. 'Oh, an' just look at me new frock.'

'Tha looks as though tha's been slaughtering a pig,' Ronald said; 'but I expect soap an' watter'll remedy that. Come on, let's see if tha can stand up straight.'

Ella let herself be helped up. As Ronald released her she swayed and staggered and Walter grabbed her.

'I'll take her home,' he said.

'Tha'll do nowt o' t'sort,' Ronald said. 'Thee make thi'sen scarce.'

'I'll take her an' tell 'em what happened.'

'If tha wants to explain tha'd better wait an' call another time. I don't know if tha's ever seen Ella's father wi' his rag out. She's bairn o' t'family, tha knows.'

'I'm twenty-one years old,' Ella said, 'and quite able to look after meself.'

'It seems like it.'

'Well, I'll do all the explaining there is to do.'

'I'm sorry, Ella,' Walter said, and he did look so abject, words of forgiveness were on her lips when Ronald broke in again:

'Tha'll happen be more careful who tha goes out wi' another time.'

'I shall go out with who I want, Ronald Palmer,' Ella snapped. 'And I'll thank you not to poke your nose in where it's not wanted.'

She realised the silliness of her words and thought she was going to laugh. But before she could laugh she began to cry, and she turned blindly away from them and, nearly going full length over one of the guy ropes, but saving herself in time, made off into the darkness of the field beyond the perimeter stalls, not caring who would follow her or that she might have to make her way home alone.

She carried the mark of it to this day. She could see it as she looked at her face in the mirror, that small bump on the bone of her nose, apparent as she turned her head slightly one way. Not that she had remained self-conscious about it – there had been more important things to worry about than that small marring of her looks – but for a time she had been afraid it would spoil what little beauty she thought she possessed.

'On the contrary,' Howard – Mr Strickland, that was – had said to her some while later, 'it gives you a kind of distinction.' But then, he had had a way with words. He could nearly always be relied upon to say the right, the reassuring thing.

Patience had talked about sending her to the doctor next day. Sugden said that providing she could still breathe through both nostrils he did not see what lasting damage had been done. When she did go to the surgery, a week later, Dr Flint shone a light up her nose, then pressed it between his nicotine-stained thumb and forefinger till tears sprang to her eyes, and said the same thing. 'If I send you to hospital, they can only break it again and

55

you might come out worse than you went in.' He told her to wait and see what it looked like when it had settled down, and if it still bothered her they would think about it again.

That was after Walter had been to the house, when she was still so conscious of it, it seemed like a blatant disfigurement. Which was partly why she was so short with him when she opened the door to a knock and found him on the step.

'Hullo, Ella.'

'Oh, it's you. What are you doing coming here without being asked?'

'I've come to see your mam'n dad; to make things right with 'em.'

'You could have waited till you'd made things right with me first.'

'Nay, if I let it go till then they might think I'm 'flaid.'

'An' you're not 'flaid, then?'

'I can only tell 'em what happened.'

'They know that already.'

She had, in fact, already absolved Walter from blame, explaining that it had all come from his sticking up for someone unable to defend himself, but what she resented was what her parents might make of Walter's coming to the house uninvited.

'Who're you talkin' to, Ella?' Patience called from inside.

'It's Walter Lindley.'

'Well, ask t'lad to come in. What're you keepin' him on t'step for?'

Ella stood aside and let Walter in as Sugden came up the yard. Sugden washed his hands under the tap as Walter began to apologise for sending Ella home in that condition.

'Her brother wouldn't let me bring her meself,' he explained.

'Aye, he came an' told us when t'pub turned out,' Sugden said.

'She never came home on her own, though, surely,' Walter said. 'He went after her.'

'Well, he must ha' thought of summat else he had to do as he passed t'pub door, like gettin' another pint or two inside him while they were still open.'

'Sugden,' Patience said, 'all that's nowt to do wi' t'lad.'

'Nowt at all,' Sugden said, ' 'xcept it'll happen learn him to do what he's a mind to do wi'out takin' advice from such as our Ronald. Are you much of a drinkin' man yerself?' he suddenly asked Walter.

'I won't deny that I enjoy the odd pint,' Walter said.

'Oh, aye; nobody's expecting thee to sign t'pledge.'

Wondering what right her father had to expect anything of Walter, Ella realised that Sugden was, as a matter of course, sizing him up; taking his measure as a possible son-in-law. As plain, she thought wryly, as with recurring self-consciousness she turned her head in the light, as plain as the nose on your face.

Walter had brought the dressing-table set which Ella had dropped in the confusion at the fair, and Patience, asking to look, appeared to be admiring it until Ella said bluntly that she did not know why Walter had bothered since the trinkets were not worth house-room.

'That's throwing kindness in t'lad's face,' Patience said.

'Happen so,' Ella said. She knew she was behaving badly but could not make herself soften, not even when, on the step as he prepared to leave, Walter said, 'I wondered if you fancied a walk. It's a nice night out.'

'I can't tonight,' she said. 'I've got some jobs to do.'

What she so fiercely resented was being moulded to other people's designs. 'If I go now,' she was thinking, 'the next thing you know he'll be here for his Sunday tea.' Then it would be every Sunday; a pattern established, an understanding assumed. And she had to have time. She liked Walter. She liked him more since the incident at the fair. She liked the spirit that had led him to take Josh Cutshall's part, and she found something oddly touching in the way he had damped down his temper and his pride and come to make things right. But why wasn't there that something extra, that hollow feeling in the stomach, the curious breathlessness that had made her careful how she spoke, which she had known with Mr Strickland? Or was all that merely her fancy; something that had grown in her imagination after she had realised she would not see him again – not her feeling for the real man, but the man she had wanted him to be?

# Four

War with Germany was declared on Ella's birthday. Her father took it badly. Sugden had known the peaceful years before 1914, when there was great disparity between rich and poor but there was a living to be made by anyone prepared to work hard, and it was possible to raise a family that was short of nothing basic to its needs. He and Patience had lost their third-born, David, in infancy. John had died of influenza in his early teens. Such losses were in the way of things. What he could not accept as natural or inevitable was that Edward's death in action in 1916 had solved nothing, that Thomas, the brother who had been a child then would now be called up to fight it all over again, and that Ronald, who had come through unscathed, would be expected to send his two sons.

Ella, now the only one of his children who saw Sugden every day and knew the pattern of those days, was troubled by the change in him. Mr Keighley, who visited them that autumn for what was to be the last time, remarked on it to Ella when they happened for a few minutes to be alone. She had come out with some scraps for the hens and found him standing looking at things before taking his evening stroll.

'Your father's very quiet these days, Ella.'

'He's taken the war very badly, Mr Keighley. It seems to have knocked all the stuffing out of him.'

'In his heart of hearts he just didn't think the world could be so stupid, I expect.'

'That's about it.'

'There was a great deal of patriotic fervour at the outbreak of the Great War,' Mr Keighley said. 'It lasted with some people for the duration, despite the appalling casualties. Some foolish young women even went about handing white feathers to men who weren't in uniform. Did you know that?'

'Yes, I heard about it.'

'I saw it happen once. It was on Euston Station. I'd gone to London on business. There were two quite well-dressed women on the platform. They were pushing white feathers into the hands of all men of serving age in civilian clothes. I was just wondering how to avoid them when they stopped a young man who had travelled in the same compartment as me. He tried to walk round them but they stood in his path. I'll never forget the look on their faces: they had a high colour and this proud, haughty expression. But they'd chosen badly. This young fellow began to shout at them so that everybody could hear. A few people hurried on – you know how most English people dislike scenes – but quite a few stopped to see what would happen.'

'What did happen?'

'He told them that he'd been invalided out of the army after being wounded at Ypres and watching his mates being killed like flies all around him; and he wished they could have been there to see it. He told them if they wanted to do something useful they ought to get into nursing uniform or go to work in a factory. He was beside himself with anger and when he stopped shouting he took the bunches of feathers out of their hands and scattered them all over the platform. Some of those looking on actually applauded him as he walked away.'

'Weren't you in the war yourself Mr Keighley?'

'I was already a bit long in the tooth for it,' Mr Keighley said; 'but I did try to volunteer in 1915, mainly because I thought it was cowardly not to. I mean for myself – I didn't judge anybody else. But I'd always had trouble with my chest and they declared me unfit.'

'Anyway, your conscience was clear.'

'Oh, yes.'

'My brother Edward joined up as soon as he was eighteen,' Ella said. 'He did it without telling me mam'n dad. He was killed on the Somme within six months. It was the year before I was born. But now there's Thomas, and Ronald's two lads. Some folk are saying it'll all be over by Christmas.'

Mr Keighley shook his head. 'I doubt that. And it's as well to be prepared. There'll be conscription from the beginning this time, too. It wasn't considered the done thing to force men into military service. Not last time. They thought they could rely on a volunteer army, as they had in the past. Hence the business with the white feathers. But that kind of thinking couldn't last in the face of the terrible casualty rate of trench warfare, and in 1916 they had to start calling men up. And once a precedent is established . . .' Mr Keighley shrugged.

'D'you think it'll be like that this time?'

'Trench warfare, d'you mean? No. I imagine it will all be more mobile. And nearer home. We shall all be in it this time, one way or another.'

The low golden sunlight of the October evening lay across the garden. Mr Keighley stirred himself out of his reflective mood and asked,

'Have you seen *The Citadel*?'

'No, not yet.'

Mr Keighley took the watch from his waistcoat pocket and snapped open the cover.

'I shall get there in nice time. I'm a great admirer of Robert Donat, you know.'

The last time Ella had seen Robert Donat had been in *Knight without Armour*, with Mr Strickland. Realizing that she might not have another chance, she nerved herself and asked,

'Do you ever hear anything of Mr Strickland these days?'

'No.'

'He'll be out of prison by now, though, won't he?'

'Some time ago, if he behaved himself.' Mr Keighley

turned away. 'I'll let you know what I think of the film.'

'Thanks.'

As he walked away Ella remembered moments from that evening when she had gone to the pictures with Mr Strickland and they had brought home fish and chips for supper. It seemed now to have been one of the happiest times of her life. But over so quickly, and gone for ever. Tonight she would wash her hair and tomorrow go to the pictures with Walter.

There were some men marching about in the park, drilling to the commands of a sergeant of the Territorials. They had neither guns nor uniform, but carried poles or long brush-handles on their shoulders and wore arm-bands with the initials LDV.

'Why should England tremble?' Walter said, stopping Ella some way off so that they could watch. 'Bloody hell! If Hitler could see this lot he'd be over here tomorrow.'

'Don't swear, Walter,' Ella said automatically. They did make a comical sight, she had to admit, but she disliked Walter's lack of respect for those ready to do their bit for the war effort.

They were mostly older men who would not be called up for active service, and some younger ones getting into practice while waiting for their papers. Local Defence Volunteers, they were. Walter said his father was among them and laughed. ' "LDV",' he said. 'Look, Duck and Vanish. That's what they'll do if the Gerries do come.'

There had been some naval casualties, but little else so far. An expeditionary force had gone to France. Ration books, identity cards and gas masks had been issued. Children were being evacuated from London and the other big cities. Some young men had disappeared from the streets and reappeared in uniform; but the call-up was generally slow and there were said to still be over a million signing on for the dole. Walter had registered and was waiting for his medical. 'What's the use of calling us up,' he would say when asked if he'd got his papers, 'when they've no tackle to give us?' 'The phoney war,' some people were calling it.

'D'you know what the RAF's doing over Germany?' Walter said. 'Droppin' propaganda leaflets. I heard a gag about that. There was this clumsy sod in aircrew who pushed a whole parcel out before it was undone. "You want to take more care, doing that," his officer says to him. "You might kill somebody." ' Walter laughed again. He seemed to be getting a lot of amusement out of the conduct of the war. But Ella knew him well enough now to detect a note of bitterness and frustration behind it.

'And what do you think the Gerries do with all these leaflets we're droppin' on 'em?' he asked.

'Read 'em, I suppose.'

'Read 'em be buggered. They prick holes in 'em and hang 'em in the lav. We're supplying the enemy with free arse-wipe.'

'You know, Walter, you have got a vulgar tongue.'

'Aye, I know,' Walter admitted. 'I don't seem to be able to help it.'

'So what would you do if you were in charge?'

'What would I do? Nay, lass, I don't know. I'm just like everybody else: I shall do what they tell me to do when they make their mind up.' He turned his back on the drilling men and look down the slope of the park, through the boundary trees and across the valley to the far hills.

'I know what I'd like to do for meself.'

'What's that?'

'Before they do fetch me I'd like to make sure of thee.'

Ella's heart fluttered. 'And how would you do that?'

'By putting a ring on thi finger.'

Her only feeling was of alarm. It was all too quick. He was giving her no time to think.

'Are you talking about getting engaged?' she managed.

'Engaged nowt,' Walter said. 'There's no time for all that fol-de-rol. I'm talkin' about gettin' wed.'

'You're expecting a lot, aren't you?'

'Oh, aye.'

She turned and took a step or two away from him. 'If we're going for a walk let's go before it drops dark.'

Some new electric streetlamps along the main road out of the town had been switched on for the first time last winter. People had wondered aloud at their brilliance. 'Just like daylight,' they had said. 'You can read t'small print in your newspaper under 'em.' But they would not be seen again for the duration. The black-out smothered everything after nightfall. People groped as though blinded along familiar streets, among buildings from which not a sliver of light escaped. Patience would not stir out of the house after dark. Women on early morning start at the mills sought the reassurance of groups and went chattering and laughing down the lanes by the dim light of blinkered torches. The one-armed lamplighter was seen no more.

As the sun went down across the valley, Ella walked beside Walter in a mounting dismay. What could she say to him? She had been keeping company with him for only a few weeks, and what he was asking for was the commitment of a lifetime. But then, lifetimes – or men's at least – could no longer be measured by normal standards. Who knew where Walter might be in six months' time? Who was to say how much she might miss him when he had gone?

Walter swung a stick broken from a hedge. They were walking now along a path by a stream, among open fields. There was nobody else about. Neither of them had spoken for a long time. She wondered if he was angry at her lack of response.

'Well, talk's free,' he said finally. 'Say summat.'

'I don't think I love you, Walter,' Ella said. 'No, I know I don't.'

He stopped and made himself face her, his colour rising. 'Eh?'

'I don't love you. I'm . . . I'm fond of you, I suppose. I mean, I must be. But I don't love you.'

'Well I love you,' he said, 'and that can be enough to be going on with.'

64

'Can it, Walter? Do you really think it can?'

'I'm ready to chance it.'

'No, but is it fair?'

'We're not at pictures now, y'know.'

'Eh?' she said, baffled for a moment.

'This is real life,' Walter said.

'Is it different, then?'

' 'Course it's bloody different, Ella. "Is it different?" You know it's different.'

'There's no need to carry on.'

'Look, lasses in real life marry chaps 'at'll look after 'em an' treat 'em right, an' then they grow to love 'em.'

'All of 'em?' Ella asked.

'Thousands of 'em,' Walter said. 'Millions of 'em.'

'I know plenty 'at's far from that. Them 'at are not scrappin' outright can't talk about owt else but scoring points an' laughin' up their sleeves when they've got away with something. I don't want to be always trying to . . . to put one over on me husband.'

'You wouldn't be,' Walter said, 'because you're not like them. And I'm not like their husbands.'

'I still don't love you, Walter. Not like I should.'

Walter dropped his stick and said, 'Come here.' he took hold of her and she found herself pressed up against him while his full red lips covered hers. It was the first time. Whenever he had offered before she had turned her face and allowed him only her cheek. She tried to relax her lips but she was off-balance and, suddenly laughing right against his mouth, she had to put one foot out behind her to stay upright without hanging on to him.

'Sorry, Walter.'

For a moment he looked at her for a sign that she was deliberately making fun of him; then he glanced round. One hand still held her above the elbow. He squeezed her as he said again, 'Come on.'

'Come on where?'

'Through here.'

There was a hole in the hedge and beyond it a small

secluded patch of grass on the edge of the beck, which just here curved so that you could see neither upstream nor down. Walter drew her through after him and stooped to feel the grass.

'It's dry.'

Thinking that any second now she would stop him, she let him draw her down then press her back until her shoulders touched the ground. He sat up then and with clumsy force struggled off his jacket, folding it and lifting her head to push it under. Still she did not resist as he lay half over her and kissed her again. But when she felt his fingers at the press-studs down the front of her blouse she twisted her mouth free to ask, 'What d'you think you're doing?'

'It's all right,' Walter said, 'I'll stop as soon as you say so.'

'I'm saying so now.'

'No, you're not,' he insisted. 'Not yet.'

She felt her face flame as her breasts were exposed to the cool air. Cool breasts, burning face. Then Walter's hot face was between them, his mouth exploring their shape, moving from one rising tip to the other, then settling and opening and searching and drawing, like a suckling child. Ella found her hand on his head, cupping, encouraging as her body melted under him. She had no use in her legs. Her thighs were slack and heavy. As she wondered at how they could usually respond to the least half-registered request of her brain, a thought came to her. They were all now at the mercy of forces stronger than themselves: she herself, Walter, everybody. If she could not make up her mind, then, whether or not she wanted him, why not let that choice out of her hands? If fate or providence or God meant her for him, the clear sign would be given her so long as she delivered herself up and opened herself to it.

Then as she lay slack and yielding, saying no to nothing at all now, Walter said something of a charm she would never on this earth have believed him capable.

'Oh, Ella,' he said, 'you're like the first woman ever made.'

But oh, what a pity, she thought, that he could not be the last man.


Patience had been washing. Ella was sweating in the day's accumulation of heat in the kitchen after her walk up from the mill. Patience waited until they had eaten their meal of cold beef, fried potato and brussels sprouts, and Sugden had gone for his evening look at the hens, before she asked, 'You haven't started your monthlies, have you?'

'No.'

Useless to say otherwise, for Patience knew well the cycle of Ella's periods as she knew every other recurring event marking off the weeks and months in the steady progress of the years.

A laden clothes-horse occupied a corner of the hearth near the small fierce fire. Patience reached out and took from it the knickers Ella had been wearing when she let Walter have his way.

'I found these under your bed. If you'd thought to wash 'em through yourself when nobody was about, you should have hidden 'em better.'

'What do you want to know?'

'Whether I'm right in what I've been thinking.'

'It depends what you've been thinking.'

'Ella,' Patience said, 'you're not a bairn any longer. Your father 'ull be coming back any time and we'd better not be talking about this when he does.'

'What if you are right?' Ella said. 'I'm old enough to do what I please.'

'Not while you live under this roof, you're not. Though I hope you are old enough to know your own mind.' Ella said nothing. 'Was it Walter Lindley?'

'Who else d'you think it might be?'

'Nobody else, unless you've learnt ways I never knew you had.'

'Well then.'

'Have you got an understanding or did he just take advantage of you?'

'He wants me to marry him, before he gets called up.'

'I see.'

'But I've told him I don't know if I want to marry him.'

'Well, it's a fine way to be undecided, letting him have all he wants with you; summat you've never given away before, and you can't take back.'

'I told him I don't love him. Not the way I ought to.'

Ella heard herself with surprise. She had not thought to say so much. Yet what could she say in the face of her mother's assumptions? Her face flamed all the more as she thought of the daft situation she had put herself in.

'It's summat we allus saved for a chap we were sure of,' Patience said. Ella thought she was doubly shocked now at the notion that she might have a daughter who was wanton enough to give herself not only before marriage but without commitment, simply because she might enjoy it. 'And I did,' Ella thought. 'I did. And I wonder if that makes me wicked.'

'I wanted –' she began, then stopped.

'What did you want?'

But Ella did not see how she could explain that urge which had come upon her, the urge to put herself in the hands of something outside herself.

'You'll happen find yourself with summat you *didn't* want, soon enough,' Patience said, when Ella did not go on.

'Well then.'

'Are you ready for that?'

'If it happens, I shall have to be, won't I?' Ella said, and Patience shook her head.

'Ella, lass. I allus thought I knew my last born as well, if not better than I knew the rest. An' I thought – though it's a thing I shouldn't say –'at you'd summat a bit finer in you than most of 'em. But you've capped me. I can't fathom you at all. You've . . .' Patience sought for words. 'You've put yourself in a cleft stick, lass.'

'That's right, Mother,' Ella said. 'Now you see it. That's just what I've done.'

But then, as so often in life, it did not happen in the way offered. The look on Walter's face when she told him was a mixture of disappointment and relief, with disappointment finally on top. For that would have secured her, and now he was once more at the mercy of her whim, soon aware that her giving herself to him bound her no more than she had been bound before. Like Patience, he was at first shocked that she could apparently have done it for no more reason than the pleasure it brought. And then, when he thought it through to a new advantage – that if she had enjoyed it once she would be ready to enjoy it again – he was baffled by her steadfast refusal to yield a second time.

'You're playin' with me, Ella,' he said furiously. 'I don't know whether I'm comin' or goin'.'

'Neither do I, if it comes to that,' Ella snapped back, tired of his badgering as she was weary of the turmoil of her own feelings.

'There's a name for women like you,' Walter muttered. Having tasted and had the pleasure withdrawn, he was now almost desperate in his need. He spoke softly into her ear on the back row of the pictures, which, now that the nights were drawing in and turning colder, was about the only place they could find a measure of privacy in comfort. 'Admit it,' he wheedled. 'Say you enjoyed it.'

'What if I did?' Ella conceded finally. 'I'm not taking the risk again, so you can just stop pestering.'

Sugden could not understand why this lad his youngest daughter was seeing so much of had not started coming for his tea.

'Happen she's not sure in her own mind,' Patience said, and later repeated the conversation to Ella.

'If she's walkin' out with him two or three times in t'week she must be sure of summat.'

'There's a war on,' Patience improvised. 'Walter doesn't know when he'll be called up and where he'll be

69

sent to. Our Ella might not fancy tying herself to a soldier.'

'There'll be damn' little else for her to tie hersen to afore this lot's over,' Sugden said. 'And she'll be a year or two older by the time it is. I'd like to see her wed, Patience.'

And Patience, knowing more than he did, said, 'So would I.'

'There's nowt wrong with her, is there?' Sugden asked on a sudden thought.

'What ever do you mean, Sugden?'

(What ever *did* he mean? Ella wondered when told.)

'I mean she wants a husband and some bairns, like most women.'

'Well, o'course she does.'

'Speak to her, then. You're her mother. Advise t'lass.'

'Oh, perhaps I was cruel,' Ella thought long afterwards. But she did not know how else to behave, except to send him away altogether, to tell him there was no chance for him at all. And how she had struggled with herself unable to rid her feelings of the possibility of *something else*, and the knowledge that the moment she accepted Walter all that would be closed to her for ever.

No, as she saw it, she had offered her life once and it had not been accepted. The choice was given back to her and Walter would have to wait.

# Five

Walter went for his medical and was passed A1. He had expressed a preference for service with the RAF, and asked to be considered for aircrew training. He began buying a magazine called *The Aeroplane* and became an expert at identifying aircraft from silhouette drawings. 'That's a Dornier; that's a Heinkel; that's a Junker 88, a dive bomber. Stukas, they call 'em. That's what they blasted hell out of Warsaw with. We've got nowt like that, though we have got some good fighter planes. How do you tell a Hurricane from a Spitfire? The Hurricane's got curved wings and the Spitfire's are a straight taper. The Hurricane's more curved in the fuselage behind the cockpit an' all. Them's as good as anything Gerry's got, only we haven't got enough of 'em. Gladiators an' Swordfish an' suchlike are obsolete. You can easy tell them 'cos they're biplanes. What's a biplane, then, Ella?'

'They've got two wings, one on top of the other.'

'Good lass!'

Besides the aircraft, Walter could reel off the names of the firms who made them: Vickers-Armstrong, Handley-Page, Hawker-Siddeley, de Havilland, Short Bros., A.V. Roe, Blackburn, Fairey Aviation, Supermarine, Gloster. He became, in fact, aeroplane mad, and though he did not think he had the education to be accepted for flying, he took it seriously enough to stop smoking, so that he would be more fit, and began eating a lot of carrots, which, since the blackout, people said helped you to see in the dark.

'In the air, Ella,' he said; 'that's where this one's going to be settled. And we're behind. They've got the edge on us. Hitler already had aircrews getting practice in Spain, before they started on Poland. So we're going to need to train a lot of men; and they can't all be public school boys. In any case, if I only get to be an aircraft mechanic I shall have another trade when the war's over.'

'Won't you want to come back to butchering?' Ella asked.

'Who knows? It's nice to have another string to your bow.'

An aircraft mechanic, Ella thought. He would not have to do any actual fighting if he became one of those. She hoped he would not be too disappointed, but it seemed to her the best, because the safest, thing for him to be.

They both saw the motor car as they came out of the ginnel. It was big and black and shiny and it stood alone in the Sunday-afternoon quiet of the street.

'Ey,' Walter said, 'who's that in a motor car at your house?'

'It's our Ada.'

A man in a black suit and a cap with a shiny peak came out of the house and got into the car. He drove off on his own.

'She doesn't have a flamin' chauffeur, does she?' Walter said.

'She doesn't have a flamin' car, even, dozy,' Ella said. 'It's her boss's. She's in service with this couple in Harrogate. Cook-housekeeper. Her husband's the chauffeur.'

'Nice work if you can get it,' Walter said. 'Running about in somebody else's car.'

'They don't get much time off. We see 'em once in a blue moon. Only sometimes, when Cyril has an errand this way his boss lets him bring Ada with him. She'll be inside now.'

Ella slowed her pace. She had softened enough to pass

72

on to Walter Patience's standing invitation to tea; but she would have preferred there be no one else present on this first occasion.

'What you stoppin' for?' Walter asked.

'Our Ada's picked up some fine ideas while she's been in service.'

'What if she has?'

'Oh, nothing.'

'You mean she might think I'm not good enough for you.'

'Why should she think that?'

'Nay, I don't know. She's *your* sister. What's so posh about drivin' a car for another feller an' hangin' about waitin' for him, at his beck an' call day an' night?'

'Nothing.'

'Well, come on, then; your mam'll be waitin' for us.'

The trouble was, though, that Ada played the lady to the manner born and echoed the opinions of her employers as if they were her own.

'Of course, it'll all be over any time,' she said as she passed one of the best china cups to her mother for a refill. 'Just as soon as the government realises that the Germans don't want to fight us again, and Mr Chamberlain makes a settlement with Hitler.'

'I thought he'd made one already 'at didn't turn out to be worth the paper it wa' written on,' Sugden said.

'What have Czechoslovakia and Poland got to do with us?' Ada asked. 'We should be uniting with the Germans against the Bolsheviks. They're the people we've got to be afraid of.'

'Chamberlain wants to hand over to Oswald Mosley, then,' Sugden said. 'He'll make your peace for you.'

'If Mosley had been in charge we'd never have got into a war.'

'If Mosley had been in charge he'd've given Hitler everything he asked for.'

'Hitler doesn't want anything from *us*, Father.'

'Is that what them well-off folk you work for tell you?'

'It's what they think, yes.'

'And what do they expect to get out of it if t'British Isles is turned into a German colony?'

'You're exaggerating, Father.'

'Am I?'

'Yes, you are. You ask Cyril what he thinks when he comes back.'

'I shall ask Cyril nowt. I can make me own mind up wi'out asking Cyril what to think.'

'You're stubborn.'

'We s'll all have to learn to be stubborn afore this lot's over.'

'And that's the pity of it. We shall all have to suffer for it unless somebody shows some common sense.'

Sugden sighed and shifted in his chair. Ada sat stiff backed at the table, cup and saucer held high, her veil turned back to allow the passage of the cup to her prim mouth. For all the world, Ella thought, like the lady of the manor visiting her tenants. Walter was stiff too, darting little glances from face to face but catching no one's eye, as he minded his p's and q's and waited for things to be passed to him. Patience had made a good table, nearly as good as Christmas, and towards bedtime there would be a supper of cold cuts from the dinnertime joint, and pickled onions. If he followed his habit, Sugden would then send round to the pub for a jug of beer. Ella wondered if Walter thought they made such a spread every Sunday teatime, or realised that the extras were for his benefit, as Patience had not known that Ada and Cyril would be calling.

'You're sayin' nowt, Walter,' Sugden said suddenly, and Walter started.

'Eh?'

'What d'you think about it all?'

'You mean about t'war an' that?'

'Aye, what we've just been talkin' about. You were takin' notice, weren't you?'

To Ella's surprise and embarrassment Walter blushed and she felt her own cheeks burn as she saw it.

'Nobody wants a war,' Walter said.

'Of course they don't,' Ada declared.

74

'But if we let Hitler take all Europe over he won't be satisfied till he's taken us over an' all.'

'Tha're reight, Walter lad,' Sugden said. 'I wish tha weren't, but tha are.'

'What does he know about it?' Ada demanded, and Ella suddenly felt that she would like to slap her face because she knew she was going to be offensive. 'I don't get my opinions from t'Co-op butcher's lad, I hear what people with influence and position have to say.'

Sugden jabbed his pipe stem at Ada before Ella could butt in. 'Well, if everybody wi' position and influence, as you call 'em – if all of them think that same road, we might just as well stop arsing about and send Hitler a Christmas card and tell him to come over an' take what he wants. But they don't, Ada, and thank God for that. And as for Walter, Co-op butcher's lad he might be, but I don't know 'at that makes him any better nor any worse than you and your Cyril. And in any case, he's a guest in this house, and it's my house, and I asked him his opinion and so he's a right to say what he thinks wi'out puttin' up wi' your slaver.' He pushed back his chair. 'Now I'm goin' outside for a breath of air.'

'Oh, dear!' Patience said as the door shut behind him.

Ada's nostrils quivered. 'Well! I don't know why he had to take on like that.'

'Your father's very upset about the war, Ada.'

'I'm upset. We're all upset.'

'So now nobody can be more upset than you are either, Ada,' Ella said; but Ada did not work that one out immediately, and Patience said firmly that they would change the subject.

Walter was looking distinctly ill at ease now, and she made no wonder, the way Ada had tried to demean him. But she thought he would look a sight more uncomfortable if he suspected for a second that Patience knew what they had been up to that time by the beck.

'If it's all right with you, Ella,' he said now, 'I'll go and have five minutes with your dad.'

75

'He's best left alone,' Patience said. 'There's a fire in the other room. You let Walter sit in there, Ella.'

Ella took Walter through and said she wouldn't be a minute; she just wanted a word with Ada.

'I didn't know you'd started courting, Ella,' Ada said when Ella went back into the kitchen. 'I expect everybody says it's not before time.'

'Don't you start jumping to conclusions, Ada, just because I bring a lad home to his tea.'

'I'm sorry I spoke, then,' Ada said. 'Good heavens! It's getting as you can't say a word in this house without getting your head snapped off.'

'You want to choose your words with more care, then,' Ella told her. 'You come flouncing in here with your airs and graces, looking down on Walter because he works in a shop. Anybody 'ud think you own that big house you live in and that car your Cyril drives. But you're only servants, Ada, and I don't know why that makes you so high and mighty.'

'When you work for the Quality you learn how to be Quality yourself.'

'If them's the sort of manners you learn from the Quality, it's time you took 'em back where they came from.'

'Ella,' Patience said, 'this is still Ada's home as much as it is yours.'

'And I'm not going to be made to feel unwelcome in it by my little sister,' Ada said.

'Then don't come here making out you're summat better than everybody else, 'cos we know you, Ada. We can remember when you used to wet t'bed.'

Ada looked flabbergasted. Her mouth opened and shut a few times before she managed, 'Well! I've never heard such . . . such tales.'

'Now don't deny it,' Ella said. 'I remember and so does our Doris, 'cos you wet us while you were about it.'

While Ada continued to flounder, Patience said, 'You did go through a funny time, Ada, after you'd left school an' gone into t'mill. You were livin' on your nerves for months.'

Having had her say, Ella did not want to hang about and appear to be gloating, so she said, 'I'll go and keep Walter company. Call me when you're ready to wash up.'

'We'll keep table laid in case Cyril wants something,' Patience said.

Ella went through to Walter. She wanted to believe what Ada had said: that the war could be settled without more fighting; but she knew little of the issues involved, and if her father did not believe it she preferred to rely on him. She would have liked to hear Mr Keighley's contribution to what had been said, and fleetingly, as she thought this, Mr Strickland came into her mind. Where was he now? Was he perhaps already in the army? Would his prison sentence have any effect on that? She thought it might interfere with his becoming an officer, and that was a pity. Mr Strickland was the officer type. She did not think Ada would have been stuck-up with him.

The arrival of Ada's husband took some of the strain out of the atmosphere. Cyril liked to unbend in his wife's parents' house. A little while after she had heard the car and seen her father walk up the yard, Ella went into the kitchen and found her brother-in-law alone at the table, in shirtsleeves and braces, tucking into a plate of boiled ham and tomatoes. Sugden, sucking on the stem of his dead pipe, had re-occupied his wooden armchair on the hearth, and Ada stood beside her mother at the sink, drying pots as they came out of the water.

'You should have called me,' Ella said.

'I can still dry a pot,' Ada said. 'Lord knows I get enough practice.'

'Well then, Ella,' Cyril greeted her. 'How are you keeping?'

'I'm well enough. What about you?'

'Occasional twinge of rheumatism. Nothing to make a song about.'

Cyril had been just old enough to serve in the army in the last year of the first war, and had then done twelve years as a regular soldier. He had the manner of a man who had mixed with men and knew his way about the world. His hair was cut severely short above his rather prominent ears and slicked back neatly along his narrow head. He sometimes sported a small moustache, but at the moment was clean shaven. His starched white shirt gleamed in the fading daylight and when he smiled he showed brilliant white dentures. Ada had been in a lowlier situation at another house when she met him, and in her late twenties when they married. They had no children, which made it easier for them to offer themselves as a husband-and-wife team. With Cyril's army pension and their wages on top of their keep – and not much time off for spending – they were able to save, and talked sometimes of their plan for the not-too-distant future of taking over a pub or a small hotel.

'Where are you hiding this young feller of yours, eh?' Cyril asked.

'He's in there.'

'Aren't we going to be favoured with a look at him?'

'He's all right where he is.'

'Oh, fetch him in. He's one of the family, isn't he?'

'Not yet, he isn't.'

'Careful, Cyril,' Ada said; 'it's a delicate subject.'

'Delicate, is it? Umm. Well, I'm sure I don't want to frighten the lad off.'

'It's not a question of that, Cyril,' Patience said. 'T'lad's willin' enough, by all accounts, but it's our Ella who's holding t'string. I sometimes think she's more faddy than our Ada was.'

'A good job Ada was faddy, or somebody might have snapped her up before I came along.'

'There was no Tom, Dick or Harry going to make a drudge out of me,' Ada said.

'No, it takes Quality to do that,' was what Ella felt like saying, but she grinned and held it back.

'And I nipped in just in time before some chap with money got his sights on her,' Cyril said. 'Wasn't I lucky?'

He said it so naturally that Ella found herself looking

at him twice to see if she could detect a trace of sarcasm. Ada obviously took it at its face value and no more than her due.

'Walter's all right,' Sugden said.

'Oh, he might be all *right*, Dad,' Ada said, 'but is he right for our Ella? If our Ella's any sense, she'll wait till she's sure of her own mind.'

Walter had started biting his nails since giving up smoking. He was nibbling at them again, standing with his back to the fire, when Ella went to him. It made him look nervous, as though he expected something unpleasant to happen, and she thought how quickly someone whom she had always considered brash could be at a loss with people, in a situation he did not understand. She herself had helped to bring him down, she knew, by the way she played him along. She had excited him beyond his wildest dreams, and now that she would neither give herself again nor accept his ring, he was plunged into sullen dissatisfaction. Perversely, now, she found herself wishing him to be more like his old self and knew it was only with her that he was not.

'Our Ada's husband's asking about you.'

'Oh aye? I've got to pass muster with him an' all, have I?'

'He knows you're here, that's all.'

'Are you going' to wait till they've all had a look at me, and taken a vote?'

'I don't know what you mean.'

'I mean before you make your mind up.'

'I can make it up for meself.'

'You're not showing much sign of it.'

'Well, I don't need them to tell me what to do.'

'I don't know about that. You're a tight family, you Palmers.'

'What d'you mean?'

'You're clannish.'

'Us? *We* are? I thought we just about put up with one another most of the time. When we're not fallin' out about something.'

79

'It's not how it looks to other fowk.'

'Who's other folk? Who's been talkin' about us?'

'It's common knowledge.'

'It's common rubbish.'

'Your Thomas clouted a feller in t'Trades an' Labour Club the other night, 'cos he'd said summat about your Ronald.'

'I didn't know that.'

'Didn't you? Well, he did. And he got himself barred for it.'

'Our Thomas has a short temper. Always had.'

'No reason to go round clouting blokes.'

'It happen is if they're talking the kind of rubbish you've just been talking. And don't forget I've seen you take your coat off.'

'You stick together,' Walter muttered. 'I'm courting you, not all your family.'

'It's news to me, Walter Lindley.'

'What is?'

'That we're courting.'

'There y'are,' Walter said. 'One minute you're down on your back givin' me all you've got, and t'next you're holding me at arm's length.'

'There's no need for that vulgar talk.'

'What wor you thinkin' about while you were doin' it, eh?'

'What I was thinkin' about is none of your business.'

'Whose business is it, then? It was me 'at was up you.'

Ella thought she would choke. She lifted her hand. If they had been anywhere else, she thought, she would surely have struck him.

'Wash your dirty mouth out before you speak to me again.'

'I call things what they are. An' I'll tell you summat else an' all. A lass what does that wi' a feller she's not courtin' is no better than a –' He stopped.

'A what?' Ella demanded.

'You know.'

'Go on, say what you mean.'

'You're just seekin' an excuse.'

'For what?'

'To send me on my way.'

Ella looked over her shoulder. The door to the other room was of tongued and grooved boards and fastened only lightly, with a simple latch. It didn't fit too well, either: Ella's mother would rarely sit in here for long because of the draught it let through, which, she always maintained, blew more strongly that way.

Lowering her voice, Ella demanded, 'Have you been talking about it?'

'Talkin'?'

'Have you been braggin' to the other lads?'

Walter straightened up, fastened the middle button of his jacket and pulled his shirt cuffs down.

'I don't know what kind of a feller you take me for, but I reckon it's time I was off where I'll be more welcome.'

'And where might that be?'

'You what?'

'Perhaps I ought to say "who might that be?" '

'I'm not short o' choice.'

'Well, nobody's keeping you here.'

'No ... right.' Walter hesitated, looked round. 'Where's your lav?'

'Outside, round the back,' Ella motioned. 'I'll get you the key.'

When she came back, Walter pointed to the other door, in the far corner. 'Can I get out that way?'

'If you like.' She went and drew the bolt and opened the door. She could not remember when it had been opened last, and she left it ajar as he stepped through. A couple of minutes later she was surprised to see him pass the window as he strode up the yard to the street. 'Well, I . . .!'

She had fetched the lavatory key back and was securing the outer door again when her mother came in.

'Where's Walter gone?'

'He's gone.'

'I saw him. Is he coming back?'

'Not as far as I know.'

'What's up with him?'

'He wanted to go, so he went.'

'What have you done to upset him?'

'Why do you think I've done anything?'

'Because he wouldn't have walked off like that otherwise. He's got more manners than to go without a word to us. And anybody can see he worships the ground you walk on.'

'I wish everybody would leave me alone,' Ella said. And then she burst into tears.

# Six

Alice Cadman leaned over Ella where she sat, feeling
strange, on an upturned box at the end of the weaving-
shed. Alice was short and squat, with brawny arms and
surprisingly shapely legs. Her bonnet was lumpy with
the curlers she wore in her straw-coloured hair. She
pitched her voice to penetrate the hum of power and the
clatter of the looms.

'How're you feelin' now?'

'I don't know,' Ella said. 'I keep goin' hot and
cold.'

'Do you feel sick?'

'No, sort of lightheaded.'

It had come over her quite suddenly. As she had wondered at it, the world had begun to float away from her
and Alice had caught and held her as she rolled her eyes
and swayed on her feet. Lucky that Alice had been passing. The gangway between two working looms was no
place for a fainting-fit.

The day shift would be over in less than an hour.
Stilled for a little while, the looms would then re-start
under other hands. The mill was working round the
clock to complete a huge War Ministry order for blan-
kets. 'They'll be rubbin' their hands,' Sugden had said,
meaning the employers, when Ella told him that short-
time working was over and they were calling back
women who had been laid off. 'They got fat on the last
war an' they'll do t'same on this one.'

'You haven't been sick in the mornings, have you?'
Alice was asking, and Ella said, 'No, why?' before she

caught the old-fashioned look in Alice's eye, and blushed. 'Don't be daft,' she muttered.

'Nay, lass,' Alice said, 'it's you we're talkin' about.'

'I had a funny turn, Alice,' Ella said. 'If you're all lookin' for a bit of scandal, you can look somewhere else.'

Alice herself though unmarried, had a small daughter of school age. Ella did not know what had happened to the chap, nor how many times Alice had tempted providence before being caught.

'Will you be all right, then, or have I to fetch Godfrey?'

Ella was about to tell her to leave her and get back to her work, when the overlooker strolled into view without being summoned. Alice had a word with him on the way back to her place, and he came at once and stood over Ella.

'What's all this, then?'

He was an elderly man, not many years off retirement, in a greasy flat cap and a khaki overall. His mouth moved constantly in a long, creased face drained of all colour, as he chewed his false teeth. Godfrey's face always reminded Ella of a comedian's she had once seen in a pier show at Blackpool. Godfrey hadn't an ounce of humour in him, but then she understood that quite a lot of comedians were miserable people in private life.

'I had a funny turn, Mr Godfrey,' Ella said. 'I nearly passed out.'

'Can't have that,' Godfrey said. 'There's work to be done. Won't get done with you sittin' here.'

'It won't get done if I tumble into me loom, either,' Ella said. She was not given to back-answering her superiors, as some of the others habitually were, but Godfrey's attitude annoyed her. She was a good worker. He must know she would not lay off without reason.

'Do you want a drink o' water, or a breath of air?' Godfrey asked. There was a film on the lenses of his glasses. Ella wanted to ask him why he didn't clean them.

'I'm going home,' she said, suddenly making up her

mind. If he had shown any sympathy she might have asked if she could go, or not gone at all but sat there till she felt ready to try to work again. But his stupidity exasperated her, as he stood there, his lips working over his dentures which, she suspected from their tobacco-stained fissures, he never took out and cleaned; a bosses' man, always ready to drive them harder to make profits for somebody else, always ready to give them notice when the profits fell. Thought the sun and the moon shone out of the bosses, did Herbert Godfrey. He liked nothing better than a visit from one of them, when he could walk with Mister Rupert, say, through the shed and show off his own little kingdom, just as if it *were* his. And if *old* Mr Lidgett paid one of his now rare visits to where his money was made for him, why, Godfrey was like a dog with two tails.

'There's a war on,' he was saying now. It was becoming everybody's stock response to every situation, an excuse for expecting you to do what you didn't want to do, and for having done what you shouldn't.

'I heard somebody mention it,' Ella said.

If the thick, creased skin of Godfrey's face could have darkened with displeasure, Ella thought, it would surely have done so then. He was not used to sarcasm from her. But all he did was twist his lips and turn away as he said, dismissing her, 'Get your coat on, then, if you're goin'. You'll be that much short o' Friday.'

Telling herself not to expect any favours in future, Ella took off her apron, put on her coat and made her way down the stone steps to the ground floor. She exchanged a word with the timekeeper as she punched her clock-card, then parted the blackout curtain. There was no light in the loading-bay and none to be seen as she reached the yard and stood for a moment to accustom her eyes to the dark. She trembled suddenly in the damp air and her ears picked up behind the beat of the mill engine the plash of river water flowing over the weir.

To Ella's left, as she came out through the big double

gates, a metalled lane led up to the main road. To her right, it ran for fifty yards or so before opening into a concreted area where, at other times, lorries backed up to take coal from half a dozen hoppers filled from above by wagons drawn along a railway line which swung away behind to cross first the river, then the canal, before it reached its other terminus in the yard of the pit whose spoil heap crouched grey among the trees of a small wood. Puffing, whistling and clanking, the neat little loco made its journeys to and fro, the dry clack of wagon buffers and the whoosh and thump of falling coal at its destination echoing in the still air of the broad valley. But there was nothing now except the hum of the mill and the occasional plash of water on the surrounding silence, as Ella set out guided by the dim ray of her blinkered torch.

She had passed the hoppers and reached the unmade lane beyond when she stopped to consider whether she would be wiser to turn back and go the longer way round, along the road. There was no moon yet, and when she looked back the way she had come she could only just make out the shape of the mill. Strange that there should be not the smallest chink of light from its walls. In normal times, after dark, it sat there with its four storeys aglow like the hull of an ocean liner.

The fresh air had brought her round. She chided herself both for committing herself to this lonely walk, and for the growing apprehension that held her there while she tried to decide whether to give in and turn back, or fight it and go on.

Then she found her legs taking her forward as she admonished herself out loud: 'Come on, now, Ella, you're a big lass to be frightened of the dark.' It wasn't as if she did not know every step of the way; as if she would not have boasted to anyone who asked, that she could have followed it blindfold. The women made jokes about it since the blackout as they stumbled along arm-in-arm, the sillier ones among them deliberately working themselves up like children playing hide and seek, when to be hunted – even by someone you knew – could balance you quivering on that knife-edge between helpless laughter and hysterical tears.

The worst bit came early: a low pedestrian tunnel, perhaps twenty feet long, cut through an embankment which carried a spur of railway line linking the line from the pit with the permanent way above her on her left.

Men felt easier when they whistled in the dark: men who were going about their lawful business. Ella could not whistle. She had never been able to. But she could sing. The women sometimes sang as they tramped along with linked arms. Simple songs that everybody could remember, like *Ten Green Bottles*. 'Ten green bottles hanging on the wall; ten green bottles hanging on the wall. And if one green bottle should accidentally fall, there'd be nine green bottles hanging on the wall.' Then one of them – Sylvia Hartley, Ella thought – had come up with a variation that made everybody laugh: 'Ten timid women going to the mill; ten timid women going to the mill. And if one timid woman should accidentally spill, there'd be nine timid women going to the mill.' And so on, till only one of them arrived.

Ella's voice came back to her off the walls of the tunnel as she groped her way in. But she felt silly and quickly gave up. It did not match her tentative step, and every note shouted her nervousness into the darkness and announced her approach to whoever might be waiting there.

In another half-hour or so the women would come this way, bunched in impregnable groups. Woe betide any lurker who tried to interfere with that lot, and never mind the song. But Godfrey's stupidity had provoked her into showing her independence, and launched her into this predicament which she could so easily have avoided, but which her self-respect now compelled her to face and overcome. Which was the more commendable, she wondered as she felt her way through the tunnel: to force yourself in spite of your fear, or not to know the fear at all? Ronald – or perhaps it was Ada's husband – had once said that it was the men without imagination who won the medals. They did not realise the danger till it was behind them. And there was going to be a lot more of that in the near future, as people found themselves up against things they had never known before.

She told herself to think of something else; but that was next to impossible when there was nothing to see except the pale dancing blob of light from her torch, which scarcely penetrated an arm's length in front of her.

Her foot came down with full weight on something soft. She felt it yield and spread under the pressure and she gave an exclamation of disgust. Emerging from the tunnel, she found that the night now seemed paler after that enclosed blackness and it was possible for her to find grass by the path on which to wipe her shoe. But she could not clean it thoroughly, and she must remember not to carry the dog muck into the house.

That, she thought, was the worst part over. And now she realised that she had no choice but to go on this way, because a five-pound note on a silver tray would not have persuaded her to retrace her steps through the tunnel.

Was it really lighter or were her eyes adjusting to the dark? Whether or not, she almost missed that little dog's-hind-leg bend which took her on to the rising path by the railway and off this track that led back to the riverside. She made her way upwards and grasped the stout timbers of the fence as she stumbled. 'Steady on,' she told herself. 'You'll get there all the surer if you don't twist your ankle.'

It was while she was standing there recovering herself, the hum of the mill left behind in a silence like three in the morning, that she heard the scrape on the ground of somebody else's shoe.

Her heart jumped. She remained very still and listened for footsteps. Nothing. It was as though someone standing not far off had shifted one foot. Someone standing, or moving through the dark with deliberate stealth. And, she realised, with the first cold creep of real fear down her spine, she had no idea where the sound had come from: whether from behind, from the track below – or in front of her.

Were they true, those stories the women told of a man hanging about as they came to and fro? Or were they, as Ella had always thought, made up by the younger lasses to give them a thrill in the dark? Was she now being as silly as they were in letting her imagination overcome her senses? She had heard nothing. No, not true. She had heard a harmless sound and transformed it into something threatening. All might seem silent to her, but if she *really* listened, if she stood there absolutely still for long enough, she would hear that the darkness held a thousand sounds.

And if she did stand there very much longer, the shift would end and the women catch her up, which would be shaming and give them something to tease her with, when her going off alone could already have won her new respect.

But oh, she wished she hadn't! She could admit that to herself, if to no one else. All she had had to do was wait three-quarters of an hour or so, and she could have walked home in company. That stupid Godfrey, getting on the wrong side of her. How did men who were so bad at dealing with people ever get authority? It wasn't as if she felt badly now, either. All that odd lightheadedness had left her. Her mother and father would wonder when she walked in what it was that could have made her break her work, lose money and lead her into the ridiculous situation she was in now, when she was afraid both to stay where she was and to go on.

When she did move, it was with the action of someone standing on the edge of water who suddenly, as though freed of decision, finds the courage to dive in. She went on upwards, feeling her calf-muscles tighten against the slope of the path and making no attempt to quieten her shoes on the rough ground. She switched on her torch, too. If there was anybody in front of her she did not wish to startle him; and if he was about honest business he would make his presence known before he startled her.

At the top of the path she turned to her left, and her feet crunched on gravel as she walked on to the bridge over the main railway line. A train was coming. Travelling fast from the west, it caught her in the middle of the bridge, and smoke billowed up over both parapets and settled to envelop her before it dispersed. As the train's rhythmic clack receded and died in the open country beyond the cutting, a renewed silence fell. Into it, someone coughed, once, not far away.

Ella froze. Then, for a moment, anger seized her.

'Who's there?' she called. 'Who is it? What d'you think you're playin' at?' There was no reply. No sound at all now. 'Are you daft or deaf or what?' Ella shouted.

Nothing. It was too much. As the last of her small reserve of courage left her, she turned and ran, making for the steps built into the vertical face of the cutting. At the top, though there would still be no light, she would be among houses. She tripped and sprawled full length. Her right knee struck the granite edge of a step. The pain made her gasp. She had dropped her torch, and as she moved she felt it roll away from her and heard it fall over the edge. She forced herself on and up, pulling on the iron handrail, her ears straining for the sound of someone ascending behind her.

Her breath was coming in painful rasps as she reached the top. She could have sobbed at the throbbing of her knee. Soon now, though, she would reach the relative safety of the streets. It was, after all, not the middle of the night; not night at all, but late afternoon, and though dark the streets would have on them people going home from work.

But she must stop to ease for a moment the pressure in her lungs. The steps were something like one-in-three. She had never come up them at that rate before. Only panic could have driven her so. Slipping her hand into the breast of her coat, she held it against her heart as she turned to face the way she had come, listening. For some time all she could hear was the beat of blood in her ears. Then, as her gaze began to focus and make out indistinct shapes in the darkness below, she thought she saw a movement on the bend, halfway down the steps.

She swung round and plunged into the blackness of the ginnel which led to the road. 'Nearly there, nearly there,' her mind chanted as she ran. 'Just round the corner and I'm there.' Her head swam. The hollows of her body were bathed in sweat. Her step faltered as her foot caught some uneven part of the ground and she lurched off-balance, her shoulder bouncing her back off the wall. She recovered herself and ran on. 'Just this last bit,' her mind said. 'Not far now.'

The cry that broke from her as she collided full-tilt with the figure blocking the ginnel was one of pure terror. She began to pound it with her fists, as hands tried to grasp her arms, and she moaned with the pain of her bruised knee as she kicked out again and again, finally finding an ankle which she hacked at with unrelating force.

'Hold on,' a voice said. A man's voice. 'Hold on, hold on. I'm not goin' to harm you.'

She knew who it was then, and she collapsed against him in a draining of energy so complete she would have fallen had he not quickly changed his hold on her and seized her under her arms.

'Is it Ella?' Walter said, but she could not reply until her sobbing had died.

Walter held her. She was vaguely aware that she must stink of the mill and her panic sweat. But he held her and stroked her hair and kissed her wet face. 'Nay, lass,' he said, and again, 'Nay, lass. Who's after you? You're safe now, lass. You're safe with me.' Still he held her, supporting her full, sagging weight, until strength returned to her legs and she could stand unaided. Then she clung to him and, lifting her face, began to kiss him in return: not with the soft brief kisses of comfort, but deep and long and with such passion she might have been kissing her life itself. As suddenly, then, she drew back, as though only now aware of what she was doing.

'What you doin' on your own?' he asked her. 'You're early, aren't you?'

'I felt off it.'

'Badly?'

'I came away. Before the others.'

'What were you runnin' away from?'

'There's somebody down there.'

'Where?'

'Behind me. Down by the bridge. I heard his feet, then he coughed.'

'Wait a tick,' Walter said. He stepped past her and started down the ginnel. Ella said, 'Don't leave me, Walter,' and hurried after him, her hand groping till it found and could clutch the back of his jacket.

Walter stood at the top of the steps and peered into the darkness.

'I thought I saw something move on the steps,' Ella whispered.

Walter remained very still and quiet, his hand grasping hers. Then all at once he lifted both hands to cup his mouth, and bawled across the valley:

'Bugger off, whoever you are.' His voice rang back off the walls of the cutting. 'Bugger off, you sneaky-arsed, yellow-bellied swine, or I'll come down there an' beat the shite out of you!'

He grasped her hand again and they listened. Nothing stirred. There was no sound except a faint rustle as a wind sprang up in the trees behind them.

'You say he coughed?' Walter asked.

'Yes. I challenged him then, but he didn't answer.'

'It was probably a fox.'

'A what?'

'A fox. Foxes cough.'

'Do they wear boots an' all?' Ella asked.

'Aye, all right,' Walter said. 'Anyway, you're safe now. Don't you ever come that way by yourself again. D'you hear?'

'All right, Walter.'

'Are you feelin' badly, d'you say?'

'I don't know how I feel now, 'xcept mucky an' sweaty.'

'You taste all right,' Walter said. He put his mouth down to hers. 'Does you good to be scared.'

'Oh, does it?' She pulled away.

'Oh, hell!' Walter said. 'You're at it again.'

'At what?'

'Tormentin'. Two minutes sin' you were kissin' me as if you couldn't help it.'

'That was two minutes since,' Ella said. 'How did you happen to be here?'

'It's half-day closing,' Walter said. 'I thought I'd come an' try an' meet you. I expected a gang of you.'

'They'll be coming up before long. What made you come an' meet me?'

'I wanted to see you.'

'Why to-day 'specially?'

'Because,' Walter said, 'I got me call-up this morning.'

Walter walked Ella home. He took her hand and pulled her arm through his and walked her home. It was quite masterful the way he took charge of her, as if he knew her mind better than she did. Only when they reached the end of the yard did he let go of her.

'You're all right now.'

She did not feel all right. Her legs had no strength in them and her knee still hurt.

'Have you somewhere else to go?'

'Not 'specially.'

'I thought you'd come to see me.'

'I came to tell you, summat, and now I've told you.'

'You'd best come in.'

'Nay,' Walter said, 'its no time o'day to come visiting. Happen I'll come back later on.'

'I'll very likely be in bed later on,' Ella told him. 'I'm blethered, Walter. I can't stand up any longer. Come in. There's nobody'll bite you.'

Patience was alone in the house. When she had heard

the story she put her hand to Ella's forehead, said she was running a temperature, and prescribed an immediate hot bath with mustard powder in it. She poked the fire, got out a big pan, filled that and the kettle with water, and settled them on the coals.

'Where's me dad?' Ella asked.

'Round at our Thomas's.'

'He shouldn't be out on his own after dark.'

'I expected him back afore now. But he's got his walking-stick and his flashlight, so he'll manage.'

'What's our Thomas been up to?'

'Oh, he was round here earlier on. He'd broken his work an' been in t'pub at dinnertime. He wa' talkin' a bit wild . . .' Patience broke of, reluctant to discuss a family matter in front of Walter. 'Anyway, your father went round to sort it out.'

'Walter's got his papers,' Ella told her.

'Oh, has he? Well, that's his waitin' and wonderin' done wi'. When do you go?'

'They want me at a place in Cheshire t'week after next.'

'Aye, well. Seein' as you're here, you can happen give us a hand.'

Ella laughed at Walter's puzzled expression.

'She doesn't mean to scrub me back, Walter.'

Patience said, 'Ella,' mildly reproving. 'I mean you can get t'bath up for us. Have you t'strength to go down an' hold a light for him, Ella?'

Ella pulled herself out of the easy chair into which she had collapsed as soon as she came in. She was beginning to ache now in joints other than her injured knee. She lighted a candle and, opening the cellar door, went down before Walter. The zinc bath hung from two six-inch nails driven into the whitewashed wall. Ella stood aside, holding up the candle, as Walter took down the bath, adjusted his grip on it and carried it up the steps. When he had manouevred it round the table and set it down on the hearth, Patience went down on her knees and wiped over its inside with a wet cloth.

Walter watched her from the back of the room. 'Well,' he said, 'I'll be going now, then.'

'Stop if you like,' Patience said. 'I'll be givin' Ella a bit o' supper when she's done. She shouldn't have a bath on a full stomach.' She glanced at Walter, who was looking puzzled. 'If you sit down there where y'are, I can put t'winter 'edge up round her. Her father'll be back afore long any road.'

Ella went upstairs and got a clean night-gown and a double-bed-size sheet out of the chest. When she came down again, her mother was pouring steaming hot water into the bath and cooling it with cold from the tap. She pushed up her sleeve and tested it with her elbow. 'It's no good if it's not hot enough to sweat you,' she said, 'but we don't want you scalded.' She sprinkled into the bath mustard powder from the tin. 'You can stir that round when you get in.'

Ella set up the clothes-horse between the bath and the table, and draped the sheet over it. She looked at Walter over the top. '*It Happened One Night.*'

'Eh?' Walter said.

'Clark Gable and Claudette Colbert,' Ella said. 'They had to share that room on a farm an' they strung a line between the beds and hung a sheet over it. Didn't you see it?'

'Oh, aye,' Walter said. 'This old couple think they're married, then find out they're not.'

Ella turned her back before beginning to undress. Even though he could see only her head and shoulders, she could not somehow face Walter while taking her clothes off. She handed her things piece by piece to Patience, who bundled them together.

The heat of the water made her gasp as she tested it with her toes. 'Go on, get in,' Patience said.

'It's scalding.'

'It won't be in a minute. It's no good just aired.'

Slowly, Ella immersed one leg to its calf, then put in the other foot and crouched for a moment before, holding her breath, she lowered her behind. She sat to the

95

waist in the water's white grip, not moving. She did not know why she always thought it white, when it had no colour, except that they said extreme cold burned like extreme heat. With each tiny movement of her legs it was as though the water reasserted its grip and threatened to lift her skin.

Patience had taken a couple of firebricks out of the oven and was wrapping them in a piece of flannel. She moved with them to the staircase door. 'I'll go and put these in your bed. Just behave yourselves.'

Ella thought afterwards that it was the warning itself that prompted Walter to do what he would never have dared without it.

She heard his voice and was startled by its nearness. 'Are you all right?' He was actually peering at her over the clothes-horse! She crossed her arms over her breasts and hissed at him: 'Do you think this is a peepshow?'

'It's "What the Butler Saw" only better,' Walter said.

'Will you get back to your place!'

'Be a sport, Ella. Let's have another look. They're nice.'

'How do you know?' Something in her wanted to laugh at his cheek. So eager just for a glimpse of her.

'I saw 'em just now.'

'That's all you will see. Now gerraway before me mam comes and catches you.'

The creak of a board overhead sent him back to his chair. It was just as well, for the next moment Ella's father came into the house. She felt the cold current of air under the screen as the door opened and shut.

'Nah then, lad.'

'Hullo, Mr Palmer.'

'What's goin' on?'

'Your Ella's feelin' off it. She's in the bath.'

'Oh, aye? Where's her mother?'

'Just comin' downstairs, I think.'

Patience walked in. 'You've been a long time.'

'It wor a long job. It's noan over yet.'

96

'You didn't settle owt, then?'

'I did for now. We s'll have to wait'n see for t'rest.'
There was a pause. Sugden was taking off his coat. 'Is
this t'latest fashion, then: young women entertainin'
their chaps on bath night?'

'Walter brought her home. She had a fright down by
t'railway. I'm goin' to give 'em both some supper when
our Ella's done.'

'A fright?'

'She thought a feller wa' follerin' her in t'dark.'

'What wa' she doin' down there on her own?'

'She wa' feelin' badly so she came away early.'

'Daft trick to do, walkin' on her own in t'dark.'

'She knows that now.'

'It was Herbert Godfrey,' Ella said, lifting her voice.
'The miserable old devil got me back up. I never thought
what I was doing.'

'Oh, Godfrey,' Sugden said. 'I know Godfrey. As well
as I want to. Anyway, get done an' let somebody else
have a look at that fire.'

The heat of the water, with the heat of the huge fire on
her shoulder and one side of her face, was making Ella
feel slightly sick. She soaped herself, then slipped down
and immersed herself. Her mother had put a folded
towel on the fender rail. She took it and got out on the
other side to dry herself, standing between the bath and
the clothes-horse screen.

'Where's me nightgown, Mam?'

Patience handed it to her round the screen. It was of
thick winceyette and reached her feet. She had made it
herself and embroidered pink and yellow flowers on the
yoke. Walter's presence made her think of the flowing,
filmy, impractical negligees some women wore in films.
They seemed to be transparent but they revealed
nothing. Meant for warmer houses than this one. Ella
had never even owned a dressing-gown. When out of
bed she was usually fully dressed. But Patience had
thought of that. She draped one of Ella's decent coats
over her shoulders as she stepped round the screen.

The clothes-horse down and sided, there remained the labour of emptying the bath. Patience began to ladle from it into the sink with a pan. When she had reduced its weight enough, she reached to drag the bath nearer the sink. Walter got up. 'Here, let me do that.' He tugged the bath of surging water across the floor, took the pan from Patience and ladled until there was no more than an inch left. Ella moved then to lift one end of the bath. When Walter had taken out all he could with the pan, he man-handled the bath, lifting it and pouring off what water was left directly into the sink.

'Tha're a very useful chap to have about t'place, I'll say that,' Sugden remarked. 'An' tha're gettin' thi feet under t'table nicely an' all. How are tha gettin' on wi' our Ella? That's t'important question.'

'As well as she'll let me,' Walter muttered.

'Aye,' Sugden said blandly, 'I expect she'll let thee chase her till she catches thee.'

'Dad,' Ella said.

'You'll want this back down t'cellar,' Walter said, holding the bath upright.

'He'll need a light,' Patience said.

Ella got up. 'I'll go.'

'You'll do no such thing. Down that cold cellar straight after a bath. Your dad'll see to it.' She passed the relighted candle to Sugden, who seemed suddenly turned in on his thoughts. 'Here, Sugden.'

Ella sat in a glow of body warmth as Patience laid the table and opened the oven door to look at what was cooking. There was an earthenware pot of rabbit stew and some jacket potatoes.

'You'll be ready for a bite to eat, Sugden,' Patience said as the two men came back into the room.

'I am,' Sugden said. 'Is t'lad stoppin'?'

'He's invited.'

'I was just thinkin' a gill o' beer 'ud help it down nicely.'

'It needs no helpin' down,' Patience said.

'Do you want me to bob round to t'pub?' Walter asked.

'Good of you to offer. Give him t'jug, Patience. I've some money here.'

'Nay, I need no money.'

'Tha does if tha're fetching for us. Give him t'quart jug, Patience, then you an' our Ella can have a wet an' all.'

Walter went off to the Masons Arms.

'Have you an' that lad patched up your understanding?' Sugden wanted to know.

'There's never been any understandin'. Not in the way you mean.'

'What's he doin' here, then?'

'He came to meet me from work. He wanted to tell me he'd got his call-up.'

'I see. He'll be wantin' to know where he stands, then.' Ella did not answer. 'Lads away from home, in a uniform,' Sugden went on in a moment; 'they get temptation put in their way. It's as well if they know there's summat waitin' for 'em at home 'at they can rely on.' He took out his empty pipe, blew through it; then, remembering they were about to eat, put it away. 'Tell him aye or tell him no, Ella,' he said. 'But don't keep him danglin' an' expect him to come knocking on your door every leave.' He coughed. His voice changed its tone as something else occurred to him. 'Have you shown our Ella that letter 'at came, Patience?'

'I'd clean forgot about it in all the fuss.' Patience took down a letter from behind a mantelpiece ornament. She handed it to Ella. 'It came by t'second post. Is that a Birmingham postmark?'

'It is,' Ella said, 'but it's not Mr Keighley's handwriting. For one stomach-churning second she wondered if it could be from Mr Strickland. But the hand did not look like a man's, and when she had opened the envelope and quickly scanned the single sheet of thick deckle-edged paper, a groan escaped her. 'Oh, dear!'

'What is it, lass?' Patience asked.

'It's from Mr Keighley's wife.'

And, of course, the second she said that, both Patience and Sugden knew the worst. She read the letter out:

' "Dear Mr & Mrs Palmer, It is with deepest regret that I write to tell you that my husband Edmund Armstrong Keighley passed away last week. The funeral was yesterday. He always spoke so highly of you and your daughter that I wanted to write to you at this sad time and thank you for all the kindness you showed him on his visits.

' "It will be a consolation for you to know that he did not suffer and that the end came very suddenly, which was a shock as you will understand but must be counted as God's blessing. I remain yours in gratitude, (Mrs) Millicent F. Keighley." '

There was a silence. It was not Sugden's habit to rush into speech. Patience said finally, 'I'd a feelin' it wa' bad news. That's partly why I let it go out of me head.'

'You were lookin' after your own,' Sugden said quietly. 'First things first.'

'*Did* you make any sense of our Thomas?' Ella asked.

An outsider, she thought, would have wondered at the apparent ease with which they accepted the news and their readiness to change the subject. But it was their way. She knew that both of them would quietly brood about it and return to it later.

'What's wrong with our Thomas?' she said, when no one answered her.

'Nowt you need trouble about,' Sugden said.

'Nay, come on, Dad, he is me brother.' And he was of her own generation, unlike the older ones. 'Me mam wa' sayin' he wa' round this dinnertime, talkin' wild.'

'That wa' beer talkin',' Patience said.

'It wa' beer loosen' his tongue an' lettin' him say what's been on his mind,' Sugden corrected her.

'Strikes me there should have been a bit more talkin' an' a bit less fist,' Patience said.

'Who's he been cloutin' now?' Ella asked.

'Who's he allus cloutin' nowadays?' Patience said.

'Winnie?'

'Aye, Winnie.'

'Well, we all know that,' Ella said, 'so what's so special about it all of a sudden?'

'If you'd seen her face like I have today,' Sugden said, 'you'd ha' known what wa' special. I don't know now if I did right in leavin' 'em together.'

'It was as bad as that, was it?' Patience asked.

'It was. I never thought I'd see a face like that on a woman, leave alone know it wor a son o' mine responsible.'

'He wa' round this dinnertime talkin' about leavin' her an' gettin' a separation,' Patience told Ella. 'Only, he's got nowhere to take his bairns and he doesn't want to leave 'em with her.'

'Winnie's a slut,' Ella said. 'Them two bairns are sickly because they're starved. She sits in front of t'fire all day, smokin' cigs an' reading library books while they run about bare-arsed in all weathers. She can't manage her money. When she gets a bit extra she spends it on gin. What she does cook – when she does – is enough to turn your stomach. Our Thomas has always had a temper. He's allus been ready with his fists.'

'It's one thing gobbin' other fellers,' Patience said. 'That's bad enough. But his own wife –'

'He's got till he's at the band end,' Ella said. 'I don't hold with him brayin' her, but he's stuck fast, isn't he? If he does leave her they'll ten to one not let him have his bairns; and if they do, who's to look after 'em while he's at his work?'

'He's talkin' about volunteerin' for t'army and gettin' 'em taken into care,' Sugden said.

'Into care?' Patience said. 'But surely . . .'

'Surely what?' Sugden looked at Patience's expression.

'Surely we're a big enough family. If they did find neglect –'

'They've only got to look,' Ella said. 'They'll find it.'

'It's a big step, partin' bairns from their mother, Ella.'

'A pity for the bairns.'

'We're past havin' a couple o' little 'uns runnin' about

101

here, Patience,' Sugden said, 'if that's the way your mind's workin'.'

'But to send 'em among strangers, Sugden.'

'Well, ask yourself which of t'others is likely to volunteer. A bloody fine sample we've raised between us, Patience lass. A bloody fine sample. An' I'm damned if I know how it's come about.'

'Nay, Sugden, I'll not have that. They're no worse than anybody else's, taken all round.'

'Our Ella here's t'best o' litter,' Sugden said. 'An' she's hardly been tried yet.'

Ella had not heard her father speak so bitterly. He was acknowledging the disappointments of a lifetime. How could it have turned out so, when they had always done their best? It was, Ella thought, in a curiously mounting fear that was almost a panic, as though they were all caught in a trap, or fashioned in a mould they could not break. As Patience took food out of the oven, Ella looked at it without appetite and fingered Mr Keighley's wife's letter.

Patience, noticing, said, 'She doesn't say what it was, then?'

'What?' Ella said, wresting back her thoughts.

'Mr Keighley.'

'Oh. No. Just that it was sudden.'

'It must have been his heart. If it had been an accident she'd have said.'

# Seven

Granville Palmer was telling his sister Catherine and his cousin Audrey Walford a joke and could hardly get it out. Ella, on her way along one leg of the U-shaped table to have a word with Walter's sister, was stopped by a family friend who had to leave early to catch a train, and heard it all going on behind her.

'There's this chap, y'see, shovellin' hoss-muck up in t'street just by a lunatic asylum, and this other chap – a looney – pops his head over the wall an' asks him what he wants it for. "Ey, what's that for?" he sez, and this first chap sez, "It's to put on me rhubarb." So the looney sez, he sez, "Oh, you want to come in here: we get custard on ours." '

Catherine said 'Pooh!', being of an age when you pulled a face at most things. Audrey giggled and Granville, laughing before he started, was so limp with it now he slid off his chair and right under the table, crawling through to emerge on the other side, his limbs still behaving as though they were made of string.

It had been at Sugden's insistence that the children were included. Ella was the last, he pointed out; and as this also might well be the last occasion on which they could all be together, he had no mind to pennypinch on the day.

Walter's mother was dead. He and his father, who was a fitter at the gas-works lived in the same yard as Walter's sister Nellie, who cleaned for them and cooked their main meal of the day. They, with Nellie's husband and their two young children, and an uncle and an aunt

103

and a cousin from somewhere Barnsley way, were the only people on Walter's side at the wedding, apart from his best man, a schoolfriend of his whom Ella had known by sight for years. Ella did not think Walter had many more relatives. She had heard him mention some cousins who lived at Crewe, but they were on his mother's side and there seemed to have been a falling-out between his father and Walter's mother's family at some time, and now they didn't bother with one another.

Ella had not delved into all that: she expected it would be made clear in time – or as clear as it could be made. Family feuds were complicated and rooted in long-standing grievances that new provocation was always likely to re-open. For the present, she was not curious. Relations inside her own family were at the moment as harmonious as she could remember them, though her sister-in-law, Winnie, had begun to sob bitterly in chapel, setting her bairns off too, until the noise they made drowned the ceremony and the parson had to stop while they were led out. Afterwards the wedding party walked across the frozen ground between the lingering banks of snow to the Co-op Hall for a cold meal, off the price of which Walter, being an ex-employee now doing his bit in the armed forces, had got Ella's father a discount.

It hadn't been much of a do, to tell the truth, Ella thought; though she was honest enough to acknowledge that it was coloured by her own ambiguous feelings. For one thing, it had been arranged much more quickly than was usual. The lasses Ella knew usually gave ample notice even of their intention to get engaged, then planned several more months for the wedding. Anything quicker than that was a sign that there was no time to lose, and Ella had no doubt that gossip would assume that the case with her. But once she had accepted Walter, they had to name a day to coincide with his first long leave, at the end of basic training, because after that there was no knowing where he might be posted, though no shortage of guesses, from thirty miles away to three thousand. Still an uneasy lull hung over everything, and the war's most active ingredient was rumour.

Then, too, the weather – or the fear of it – had stopped some people from travelling. It had become, since Christmas, the worst winter of the century, in which rivers had frozen and blizzards had brought several feet of snow; so that – for weeks it seemed now – people had made their way about along paths cut through snow of table-top depth and more, and spears of frozen water hung from gutterings to glint and flash on those few clear days when the sky was an unbroken blue and bodies suddenly steamed with heat inside extra layers of clothing donned against yesterday's raw fog and frost.

But Ella's awareness that she had somehow failed to make the most of a day she expected to experience only once in her life was mixed with relief that it had not been bigger or fancier. For she feared that anything more elaborate might only have magnified her lingering doubt into naked panic at the sham she was acquiescing in. How many brides, she wondered, doted unreservedly on the man they stood beside at the altar? How many more were nagged by the thought that they might be making a mistake they would have to live with for the rest of their lives? And which of them in the end found they had made the most durable and fulfilling marriages?

'Give us a smile, then.'

She managed a small one for Walter, who, wearing his blue uniform which had not yet settled to the shapes of his body, sat in the opposite window-seat of the empty compartment as the train clacked up the winter valley and into the white Pennines.

'You were miles away.'

'I was just having a little think.'

'What about?'

Her impulse was to ask him if he thought his ring on her finger gave him a right to share everything that passed through her mind; but instead she asked:

'Have you ever been to Blackpool out of season?'

'No.'

There had been nowhere else they could think of. Someone had even suggested London; but neither of them had ever been there and it was too big, too strange, too far away. And suppose real air raids started? Blackpool should be safe enough, and it was familiar. Or it was in season. Now Ella wondered what they would find, and had a vision of a journey across a snow-covered plain to a totally dark town, with miles of deserted promenade and a churning sea the colour of forgotten milk.

'It'll be cold,' she said. 'And there'll be no shows on, except the pictures.'

'We'll keep warm,' Walter said. 'And we'll find plenty to do.'

She caught the tail-end of his twinkle and then, as he glanced out at the darkening snowscape and back again, the sudden shyness as he waited for her reaction.

'You can't do *that* for a week.'

Walter grinned. 'I'll tell you better after.'

She found herself blushing. Apart from that one time by the beck, Walter had hardly been allowed to lay a finger on her; yet here she was, committed to sharing his bed for the rest of her days. She supposed there were some girls who were eager, and wondered if there was someone somewhere who could have kindled eagerness in her. An image of Mr Strickland slipped into her mind and she resolutely tried to banish it. She could not spend her wedding day thinking about another man. She would not. But still, as she looked out of the window, a picture of Mr Strickland in his white shirt and dark suit, as he had stood with her outside her house, persisted between her and the snow-etched shapes of sheds and broken fences and rusting scrap. Railways always took you through the backside of everywhere: you saw the worst before you saw the best.

The snow seemed to prolong the fading light. They would arrive in the dark. Blackpool was summer and crowds and lights and noise. It was as though, once the Illuminations were finished with, a huge blanket was thrown over the town and it went to sleep till June. The thought intensified Ella's feeling of unreality, of having been lifted out of normal life on to a tide of events over which she had no control. She recalled a moment during the wedding tea, with the youngest rushing about and burning energy, Ada queening it at one end of the table in lilac *crêpe-de-chine* and a new hat with both artificial flowers and a veil, and everybody taking it all for granted: a moment when she had seemed to inhabit a separate stillness as the thought came to her: 'So this is how it's happening to *me*.'

'What was your Thomas's wife roarin' about?'

Walter had asked that before, but he had a way, when he did not get an answer that satisfied him, of leaving a question and asking it again later, as if for the first time.

Again, Ella said, 'Weddings take some women that way.'

'Nay,' Walter said, 'she sounded heartbroken.' When Ella did not respond, he asked, 'Doesn't your Thomas treat her right?'

'I sometimes think Winnie's not all there,' Ella said. 'She lets things go and it drives our Thomas mad.'

'He's not famous for his patience.'

'Well, no,' Ella conceded. 'But she's not much help.'

'Does he bray her?'

Ella sighed. 'Sometimes. When things get too much.'

There was a silence.

'Well, I'm not that sort,' Walter said.

'I never thought you were.'

'I'm just tellin' you. I shall never raise a hand to you.'

'I'd like to see you try.'

'I'm just *tellin'* you,' Walter said. 'But I shall expect you to be right with me. Don't think I'm a doormat.'

Ella had to laugh at that. She pushed the square box in its leatherette case containing her gas-mask along the seat as Walter moved across to sit beside her. It was none too warm in the carriage and she was glad of his closeness as he drew her to him and she settled her cheek against the rough nap of his tunic.

'I'd be the happiest chap in England,' Walter said, 'if there wasn't a war on and I hadn't to go away again.' Ella squeezed the hand that held hers. 'An' if,' he went on, 'if I thought you felt about me like I feel about you.'

'We're married, Walter,' Ella said. 'I'm your wife.'

'Aye.' He shifted his position slightly and settled himself again.

'I shall have to stop all this,' Ella thought, ' – this weighing things up – and get on with living each day.'

The train entered the long tunnel. When it emerged on the other side of the mountain, the only thing that told her they were not still in there was the snow stretching away into the thickening darkness. For night had fallen and there was not a single prick or glimmer of artificial light to be seen.

'Front door locked at eleven,' Mrs Cheetham warned them as, after their late high tea of fried Fleetwood cod with chips, tea and bread and butter, Ella and Walter were leaving the boarding house behind Central Station for a stroll as far as the promenade and a breath of sea air.

Blackpool was busier than they had expected. The war was bringing prosperity to the resort's landladies, though it would not show itself, as it did in summer, in crowded streets of holiday-makers: the incomers directed here because of the town's safe location and its abundant accommodation – servicemen in training, some thousands of civil servants moved out of London – had work to do during the day. Mrs Cheetham said that if this continued she would give up the casual holiday trade until the war was over. Ella and Walter were lucky, she said, that she had been able to fit them in. Strangers in their place she would have turned away. But Ella's letter had arrived just in time, and she could not find it in her heart to refuse someone whose family had been coming to her for years; and in the circumstances she was sure they would be quite comfortable in the attic room at the top of the house, as their legs were young enough to manage the three flights of stairs.

'She's coining it,' Walter said as they walked along the dark street of bay-windowed houses. 'She's laughing.'

'It looks like it,' Ella said. She tripped over the raised edge of a flagstone and Walter grabbed her and pulled her arm closely through his.

'You've been here a time or two before, you say?'

'Oh yes.' Though somehow now, even with the warm memory of two or three childhood holidays still vivid in her mind, Ella had found that she did not care much for Mrs Cheetham. 'Our Thomas came on his honeymoon here. So did our Doris.' After a moment she added, 'Our Ada went to Torquay.'

Always, except in heavy rain or mist, the first sight of Blackpool had been the Tower poking up its steel finger across the flat West Lancashire plain. Now their first glimpse of it was as they stood with their backs to the promenade rail while the sea at high tide surged and dashed itself at the wall behind them, and they craned their necks to look at it soaring directly above, 520 feet into a sky which, after the pitch blackness of late afternoon, had lightened with the rising of the moon.

'Can't say you're at Blackpool till you've seen the Tower,' Walter said.

No, but now that they had seen it what was there left to do?

'Would you like a drink?'

'Go into a pub, y'mean? I don't think I'd fancy that.'

'There's pubs an' pubs,' Walter said. 'I'm a bit dry.'

'Mrs Cheetham'll likely give us another pot of tea if we ask when we go back.'

'Ella . . . you're on your honeymoon, lass. There's a Yates's Wine Lodge I've heard tell about here where they sell draught champagne.'

Ella had never tasted champagne, draught or bottled, nor set foot in a Yates's Wine Lodge; but she was eager for neither. 'Let's walk a bit.'

'Suppose I take you back to Mrs Cheetham's, then pop

out on me own for an hour?'

Ella stopped. 'You what?'

'I'm on'y kiddin'.'

'I should just hope you are.'

They strolled on, walking south. Sea spray settled on their faces. It was cold.

'I could murder a pint, though,' Walter said.

'Since when have you been so fond of your beer?'

'I'm not "fond" of it. Not like you mean. But I'm parched an' a drink 'ud relax us.'

'Would it?'

'An' give me a bit of Dutch courage.'

'What do you need Dutch courage for?'

'What d'you think for?'

'Walter Lindley,' Ella said, stopping again, 'I never thought I'd see the day you'd own up to a thing like that. You're not trying to tell me you're scared of me, are you?'

'Well I –'

'After the way you pulled me into them bushes that time?'

'After the way you've kept me at arm's length ever since.'

'But we're married now. I'm your wife.'

'We've stood in chapel, and you're wearing me ring.'

'I'm not catching the next train home, y'know.'

They had manoeuvred round each other in the room at the top of the house which was almost filled by the high double bed, taking turns to wash at the basin, but not removing any clothes but top coats, and only touching when they brushed in passing. Ella had hardly expected Walter to try and take her there and then; but for him not to have offered even a cuddle and a kiss . . . And she had not felt able to make the first move. Yes, perhaps a drink would relax them both.

'If we could maybe find a nice place, an hotel or something,' she said now, 'I wouldn't mind a port and lemon. Only, you can't tell one place from another in the blackout.'

'Let's try over there.'

Walter led her across the empty tram tracks and the road. 'It looks shut to me,' Ella said as they stood before the columned portico. 'They're closed for the winter.'

'Not on your life,' Walter said. 'Not with all them servicemen and civil servants. They'll have their top brass billeted in places like this.'

'I hope they've learned you how to salute properly, then,' Ella said with a giggle as Walter marched up the steps. He turned and motioned as the door opened to his pressure.

Through a second door and they were in the chandeliered light and warmth of a lobby, with thick carpet under their feet, an unattended reception desk with room keys hanging behind it and a wide staircase. Ella caught the faint scent of cigar smoke, as though someone had walked through the lobby a moment ago. They were standing listening to the murmur of voices from somewhere they could not see, when a young lad in a chocolate-brown uniform with brass buttons suddenly appeared from under the stairs and, seeing them, turned from where he was going to speak to Walter.

'Can I help you, sir?'

'We was wonderin' if your bar's open,' Walter said.

'You're not resident?'

'Beg pardon.'

'You're not staying here?'

'Oh, no. Does it matter?'

'No, sir.' The lad pointed. 'It's on the right, through there.'

'I say.' The lad turned again. Walter stepped closer to him. 'It's not officers only, is it?'

'Oh no, sir.' Ella thought she caught the ghost of a smile on the lad's face as he went off again.

'What did you ask him that for?'

'Because when you get into the forces, Ella, you find there's places where your money's not as good as anybody else's any more.'

His earnestness made Ella smile. She slipped her arm through his. 'Well, they'll never see me better dressed.'

111

She gave him a gentle little push. 'Go on, then; let's get that thirst of yours satisfied.'

The bar was all oak panelling and brocade chairs and wall lights. There was a piano in one corner, a baby grand, and not many minutes after they had settled at a table a man who, Ella would have wagered her last pound, dyed his hair came in and, all debonair in dicky-bow and dinnerjacket, began to play. He had a light touch, not a bit like a pub pianist, and he ran through a programme including *Somewhere Over the Rainbow*, *Some Day My Prince will Come*, *I'll Be Seeing You* and *Thanks for the Memory*, letting himself go a bit right at the last, when the barman flashed the lights for Time, with *There'll Always be an England*, though, of course, nobody here joined in and sang.

Ella loved it, though she wished both of them could have felt a little more at home there. They said very little, and when one of them did speak it was in a low voice that the other had to lean close to hear. Walter had gone directly to the bar counter when they first came in, and had been sent to their table to order from the waiter, who wore a white linen jacket and presented your change on a silver-plated tray. Ella had an idea you were supposed to leave a tip, but she did not mention it to Walter. As it was, he finally asked the waiter if he could buy the piano player a drink, and when the man had been and come back to say he would have a gin and tonic, Walter said as he threw two half-crowns on the tray, 'Have one yourself.'

Three port and lemons, Ella thought. 'Three port an' lemons an' I'm his; four port an' lemons an' I'm anybody's,' one of the women at the mill had once said. She had not remembered that until the third one that Walter insisted on buying her was at her lips, and the gentle glow had spread from her abdomen into her groin. The woman in the tweed costume and pearls who had looked them over when they first came in and, smiling, leaned over and said something to the man she was with, looked

112

and smiled again as they got up to leave, and Ella became suddenly aware of the curious weakness in her knees. She corrected herself quickly, though, and got out without showing herself up.

Three port and lemons, and then she had short-changed Walter, undressing quickly and settling herself under the bedclothes while he was a floor below, in the lav. Afterwards, she had lain awake for a time while Walter slept soundly, his head against her shoulder. How he had slept, so deep and calm and satisfied; hardly moving the whole night through. Dear Walter . . . What a curious mixed blessing it was, this power to make someone happy.

Now with the curtains drawn back and the grey morning light seeping into the room, Ella stood at the wash-basin, her nightgown down to her waist, and washed her face and shoulders and breasts, the soft plash of the water the only sound in the new day.

A shifting of weight in the bed took her head half round. Walter, on one elbow, was watching her. She smiled without speaking and as she turned away again and leaned in over the basin to ladle handfuls of water over her soaped skin, the mirror gave her his rapt face as it was giving him the exposed front of her body.

'What are you starin' at?'

'You.'

As she reached for the towel, he swung his legs down and stood behind her, his arms pinioning her as his hands dipped into the water before his soaped palms began to wash her again, lifting, kneading, separating flesh that seemed to mesmerise him, as all the while his eyes feasted on what the looking-glass showed him and she, her eyes closed, pressed her head back into his shoulder and burning colour flooded her face and throat: a colour which, she realised with a small feeling of shock and the faintest echo of residual shame, was, for the moment at least, that of something very close to happiness.

# Eight

In the ten days of Walter's leave left after the honey-moon, they did the rounds of Ella's family, accepting a cup of tea and a piece of cake or a biscuit in each house. They combined their visit to Ada and Cyril with a day in Harrogate, where Ella observed with the wonder of someone set down in a foreign country the ivy-covered hotels and houses big enough to be hotels round the open expanse of The Stray, on which, here and there, the snow had receded to leave patches where clusters of snowdrops and early crocus showed against the green.

Walter tagged patiently along while Ella window-shopped up and down the streets of the town centre, exclaiming at the elegance and the cost of the clothes on show: where, that is, they were not afraid of disfiguring their displays with anything so vulgar as a price ticket. Ada and her husband lived in a flat in their employer's house that could be reached by a private door and stair-way; but first you had to enter the grounds, and for the minute or two they were exposed there Ella quite expected to be challenged and asked what they were doing. Ada served them fishpaste sandwiches with the crusts cut off and fancy buns on plates of thin china. As Ella washed her hands with scented soap in the adjoining bathroom before leaving, and thought of the chintz-covered armchairs and the view from the window, she was no longer surprised that Ada felt a sense of coming down in the world again when she went home; though she still thought it a serious flaw in her character that she made it so plain.

Ada did not encourage visits from her family. Her employers did not care for young children, she said. But something had moved her to invite Ella and Walter. Perhaps she thought there was still hope for Ella in lifting herself above the manners and attitudes of her class, while the others were now beyond redemption; though she had jeopardised her chances by marrying Walter and could, with patience, have done better for herself. Ella found herself imagining how Ada might have sucked up to someone like Mr Strickland, charmed by his manners and bearing; and chided herself for spending time on it and so diminishing Walter by the comparison.

Outside again, Walter ran his finger round the inside of his collar and drew a deep breath. 'I thought every minute I was goin' to tumble over summat,' he said. 'There's no more of 'em like that, is there?'

'No, our Ada's the only lady in the family.'

'That's where you're both wrong,' Walter said. 'You're the real lady; she only thinks she is.' He took her arm as they walked back through the town to the railway station.

'A bit of a change from your Thomas an' Winnie's, though, I must say.'

A wish to be fair had made Ella steel herself to facing with Walter the squalor of Winnie's house, and she had warned him that if he found it too much he need only make a signal and they would leave. But given a bit of notice Winnie had made an effort and was pathetically glad they had come, though awkward and shy throughout the visit. Poor feckless Winnie, whom Thomas had to live with in that three-roomed cottage of flaking stone and sagging roof. Winnie, so hopeless with money, who could spoil the plainest dish by over- or undercooking it; who always had kiddie's clothes drying on the fireguard and never seemed to get straight, letting it all overwhelm her. Tender hearted, accommodating Winnie, who, Ella now saw with the insight her own marriage had given her, had won

Thomas with a sexual complaisance that could no longer compensate for her shortcomings, leaving Ella's brother to smoulder, then erupt into ever more terrible rages.

Ella had put Walter right on the family tree. He already knew quite a lot of it, of course. 'Well, there's your Ronald and your Wilson –'

'Hold on a minute; you're missing some out. Our Ronald was the first-born. But then there was Edward. He was killed in 1916. Then there was David, who died at twelve months. *Then* there was Wilson, then Ada, then John . . .'

'John? What happened to him?'

'He died in the 'flu epidemic, in 1918, the year after I was born. After John there was Doris, then Thomas, then me. There's a six year gap between our Thomas an' me an' I've an idea I came as a bit of a surprise: me mam was carrying me when our Ronald married Martha because they'd started James. Me mother wouldn't think that decent – I mean her givin' birth at the same time as her daughter-in-law. Or she wouldn't think other folk would find it decent; which more or less amounts to the same thing.'

'Six left out of nine,' Walter said.

'Aye, and a right mixed bunch we are. Who'd think our Ada belonged to the same family as our Thomas? Or our Doris, for that matter. *She's* not as particular as she might be.'

What had struck Ella was the subtle change in people's attitudes towards her, including her mother's, in the short time since her marriage. Marriage had initiated her into a new group and given her knowledge and wisdom previously denied her; though there were hints that this was still a probationary period and full membership would only be achieved through motherhood.

'Six out of nine,' Walter said again. Then, 'I wonder how many we shall have.'

'Well, not nine,' Ella said. 'Nor six either, if I've got anything to do with it.'

'Tha'd better have summat to do with it, lass,' Walter said, 'or we shan't be having any.'

'I'm not doin' owt to stop it now, am I?'

'No, you're not, love.' He pressed her arm and grinned.

And somehow or other she could not bring herself to say that it would be wiser if they did, because they did not know how long the war would last and how much he would be away; because she did not know how her parents at their time of life would manage with a baby in the house; because she wanted to go on working for a while and save the money to furnish their own home; because, though determined to settle herself to the fact of her marriage, she was not yet ready to accept on top of that restriction the further one of a child.

'The trouble is, I'm so flamin' ignorant,' she thought irritably; and she did not know who to go to for advice. 'They see you off on your honeymoon and expect you to come back knowing everything they've never bothered to tell you.' She could not see her discussing it with her mother, a woman who had so let nature have its way she had carried nine and slipped up in her forties. And all she would get from Doris, she suspected, was that she should let things happen as they would and, when she had had enough, withdraw her favours. As for Winnie, there had been dark hints of her getting rid of one with hot baths, gin and some old wives' concoction whose name and ingredients Ella had never got clear.

No, there ought to be something she could do for herself, without spoiling Walter's pleasure. Without, if it came to that, even telling him until they were both of the same mind and could see clearly what the future held for them.

Ella found herself talking about it to Daisy Marriott one day after Walter had gone back off leave. They were walking home from the Saturday morning shift at the mill and had fallen a little way behind the others. Daisy was a fair-haired woman, small boned and plump, with a dry way with her that Ella had always liked. Though a good mixer and popular, she always seemed to keep just that bit of distance. Daisy had two children from her first husband, who had been killed in a foundry accident, but none by her second. Since she was only in her late thirties she wasn't likely, Ella thought, to have given up sexual relations.

'I thought lasses from big families learned everything young,' Daisy was saying.

'You pick things up as you go along, and this happens not to be one of 'em.'

'You don't think you're pregnant already, do you?'

'I wouldn't be asking you if I did, Daisy. I started me monthlies before Walter went back. He wasn't right pleased about it.'

'I don't expect he was. There'll be a lot of that happening from now on: fellers gettin' a spot of leave and comin' home to find their wives wi' their towels on. It's a pity t'government can't do summat about it. It'd work wonders for the war effort.'

They were climbing the rough path alongside the railway. Ahead of them, Olive Sims and a couple of others were standing waiting, one of them waving her arms about as she spoke. Olive, a thin lass with buck teeth and glasses, though not bad looking when you'd got used to her, was one of the newsiest women at the mill and sex-mad with it, while pretending she thought it all disgusting. She and some others had tried to get Ella to talk about her honeymoon, but she had refused to be drawn.

Daisy saw them too, and stopped and held on to the fence while she took off her shoe and rapped it against a post.

'Have you got a stone in it?' Ella asked.

'I'm just givin' yon' lot a chance to move on,' Daisy said. Her stocking was darned. She gently massaged the bunion by her big toe.

'Was he disappointed you weren't pregnant?' she asked.

'He didn't say so.'

'Haven't you talked about it?'

'Only about how many we'd like. But not when.'

'They'll come when they're ready, unless you do summat about it.'

'I know that, Daisy. That's why I'm askin' you.'

'There's things he can use.'

'Them rubber things? He might not want to. Don't they spoil a feller's enjoyment?'

'Oh, nowt's perfect,' Daisy said. 'But if the Good Lord made owt better he kept it for himself.'

'Do you really think so, Daisy?'

'I do,' Daisy said. 'Mind you, at my time o' life once a week's more likely than twice a day.'

'Twice a day . . .' Ella breathed. She looked up and caught Daisy's grin.

'They've gone.' Daisy slipped her foot back into her shoe and they trudged up the slope.

'What do you think I ought to do, then, Daisy?' Ella persisted. 'Walter's next leave might be embarkation, but all t'same I'd like to feel safe.'

'Don't worry about it,' Daisy said. 'I'll bring you summat to work on Monday.'

'Oh, thanks, Daisy.'

'They're summat you use yourself and he need never know about it if you don't want him to. That's between yourselves.'

'They're summat safe, are they, Daisy?'

'They're not foolproof,' Daisy said, 'but they're safer than trustin' to luck. If you want summat foolproof you'd better use aspirin.'

'Aspirin?'

'Aye, you take an aspirin tablet to bed with you and hold it between your knees.' Daisy's sudden grin lit her face. She put her head back and laughed.

It was in that first spring of the war that things began to get serious, Ella remembered. It was not the kind of remark you would make near a merchant navy man or anyone who had anything to do with the *Royal Oak*, sunk by a German U-boat in its own base at Scapa Flow; but until now it had mostly seemed half-hearted, like lads who square up to each other and neither seems to want to strike the first blow. For a while it even looked as if it

119

might fizzle out. Ada said on one of her visits that her boss had told them that secret negotiations were taking place and a peace treaty would be signed. Patience was apt to give credence to what Ada told them, her being close to people of quality; but Sugden said we had been through all that with Mr Chamberlain. Mr Churchill was Prime Minister now, and what was the point in declaring war to show Hitler he couldn't do as he liked and then backing down before anybody had struck a bat? Ada came near to calling her father a war-monger then – at least, that was how Sugden construed it – and he turned pale as death and went down the garden before he lost his temper with her.

'This war's sluffened your father, Ada,' Patience told her. 'He doesn't say these things because he likes saying 'em.'

'All I can say,' Ada said, 'is wait and see.'

They hadn't long to wait. The Germans invaded Holland and Belgium. Newsreels showed Stukas pulverising Rotterdam. Next, it could be London and Birmingham; perhaps even Sheffield and Leeds. There seemed to be no stopping the Germans now they had started. Caught out by the sudden surrender of the Belgian Army, the British Expeditionary Force retreated to the coast, at Dunkirk.

By this time Ella was a grass widow. Walter had been home on leave again, nearly bursting with excitement. He had been selected for aircrew training. He was to be sent to Canada and would be away a year.

'A year!'

'Aye, I know, lass. I shall miss you. But they can't keep shuttling fellers back'ards and forrards across the Atlantic for weekend leave.'

But a year . . . Ella had never measured such a length of time stretching into the future. She would have only the old routine to mark its passing, while Walter was diverted by the novelty of new surroundings, exacting work and the pursuit of his ambition. He was like a dog with two tails and, though Ella didn't know whether he ought to, because careless talk cost lives, he could not resist telling almost everyone they met: 'I'm off to Canada, for aircrew training.' The lad from the Co-op butchers learning to fly aeroplanes! In his excitement he seemed to have forgotten what it was all in aid of.

Ella had the most horrible dream. A nightmare. It was a mixture of *King Kong* and the newsreels of the bombing of Rotterdam. A gigantic Walter straddled the pinnacle of Blackpool Tower with her cowering in one hand. With the other hand he plucked diving Stukas out of the sky. It was still terrifying when Mrs Cheetham appeared to tell them that the lift would stop running at eleven. For Walter, riddled with bullets, finally keeled over and Ella began to fall. She woke up drenched in sweat and shouting. When her heartbeat had slowed she dragged off her wet nightgown and threw back the heavy bedclothes and lay naked in the cool night air. Not with any wanton intent that she knew of, either. Not just then. Only when, after some moments, Walter's comforting hands fired her flesh did she pull him on to her with a greed that made her face flame later, writhing and straining under him without a care for the parents sleeping – or surely now listening – beyond the thin partition wall.

'By God, Ella!' Walter whispered. 'By God, lass!'

And well he might say so. She hadn't known she was capable of it. What, he might be forgiven for thinking, would she do if she was taken like that while he was away? Not a week or two, or a few months even, but a year. At least, where he was going he wouldn't be shot at. He wouldn't be like those poor lads caught on the open beaches: queueing in patient pairs across the sand and into the sea itself as they waited for anything that floated to take them off; waiting for any boat big enough to cross the Channel and pick up a few men. And pick them up they did; they took them off; they brought them home. Thousands of them. People began to call it a miracle.

Now *that* was when men in civvies with LDV

armbands began to drill with anything that resembled a weapon, not earlier; because now was when a German invasion turned into a distinct possibility. No one would have thought of that before. Before, there had been a popular song, with a jaunty tune that soldiers could march to and cheeky words for them to sing:

We're going to hang out the washing
On the Siegfried Line
Have you any dirty washing, Mother dear?
We're going to hang out the washing
On the Siegfried Line
If the Siegfried Line's still there . . .

Nobody sang it now. Instead, they gathered round their wireless sets and listened to the sombre yet curiously uplifting speeches of Mr Churchill:

'. . . Even though large tracts of Europe and many old and famous states have fallen or may fall into the grip of the Gestapo and all the odious apparatus of Nazi rule, we shall not flag or fail. We shall go on to the end, we shall fight in France, we shall fight on the seas and oceans, we shall fight with growing confidence and growing strength in the air, we shall defend our island whatever the cost may be, we shall fight on the beaches, we shall fight on the landing grounds, we shall fight in the fields and in the streets, we shall fight in the hills; we shall never surrender, and even if, which I do not for a moment believe, this island or a large part of it were subjugated and starving, then our Empire beyond the seas, armed and guarded by the British Fleet, would carry on the struggle, until, in God's good time, the new world, with all its power and might, steps forth to the rescue and liberation of the old.'

Evening sunlight slanted into the room. No one spoke. Sugden sucked the stem of a dead pipe. Patience sat with sewing forgotten for the moment in her lap. ' . . . we shall fight with growing confidence and growing strength in the air . . .' Walter had gone to get ready to do his bit there and she, Ella thought, might as well prepare herself to do hers. This was no time to be turned in on herself haunted by vague misgivings and longings. It was a time to look outwards, to join herself to the corporate will of a people united in one purpose – to survive; a time to look and see what was to be done and do it as best she was able.

The silence lengthened. There was no sound from the street. Ella was seized by the notion that the entire country had stopped in its tracks to listen to Churchill's words and was now, like herself and her parents, sitting silently thinking them over. She had no doubt that a prayer or two was being said, and though she was not a particularly religious girl she found her mind shaping a few words. A strange grave lift of the spirit stole over her. Her father cleared his throat and Patience's hands fumbled for her sewing a second before she looked down.

'Well,' Ella said, 'he knows how to talk. I'll say that much for him.'

'Aye,' Sugden echoed, 'he knows how to talk.'

Part Two

# Nine

Mildred Sadler-Browne had killed the pigeon which Ella clapped out of their garden. The one barrel of the shotgun fired on the other side of the wall sent her on to her knees among the raspberry canes where she was gathering the first of the summer's soft fruit. She was brushing soil off her stocking when the hard, confident voice hailed her.

'Hope I didn't make you jump.' Mrs Sadler-Browne leant with her forearms on top of the high stone wall as she looked at Ella. She kept a box or somesuch permanently placed so that she could step up and talk to anybody who was in the garden. Mostly it was Ella's father. They had conversations from time to time on all manner of subjects, from foreign travel, about which Sugden knew nothing, and gardening, about which he knew a great deal, to world affairs. 'One for the pot, that. Any more bothering you, just send them over to me.'

Ella had a suspicion that the pigeon had been ringed, but she did not like to ask.

Their neighbour fished a loose cigarette from one of her pockets and lit it, picking a piece of tobacco from the tip of her tongue as she inhaled. There was a hole in the right elbow of her green jumper, Ella noticed. She was a well built woman in her late thirties. Her dark hair was cut nearly as short as a man's. Though Ella couldn't see, she was ready to bet that Mrs Sadler-Browne was wearing trousers, probably of corduroy. She could remember seeing her in a skirt on only a couple of occasions, one of them her wedding day. They had all been a little surprised when Mildred Sadler, who shot and swore like a man, had married; less so when Mr Browne, a stranger to them, had almost immediately left for foreign parts, to be rarely seen since. The local paper had said he was a botanist who travelled the world collecting rare plants and flowers, which was probably how he had come to meet Mildred, through her father. For old Mr Sadler, bought out of his share in the family wool business – in which he had never shown much interest – had been a great traveller himself, his speciality being not plants but photography.

There was an older, married brother, who lived some-where else, and Ella thought that the three people left must rattle round that big house like peas in a drum: direct, forceful Mildred, her mother, a slip of a woman with an abundance of whitening hair gathered untidily under a hairnet, and her father, who always wore a pointed come-to-Jesus collar and a black jacket, or a linen jacket and Panama hat in warm weather, his eyeglasses dangling from a ribbon round his neck and the inevitable cigarette, which he rarely removed from his mouth till it was ready to burn him, sticking out from under his grey, nicotine-stained moustache. Ella had never seen the inside of the house, but Ada had got her first taste of domestic service there when she supplied an extra pair of hands to those of the housekeeper and the daily maid on special occasions.

Mrs Sadler-Browne eyed the spilt raspberries which Ella was putting back in the basin.

'Good crop there, by the look of it. Going to make jam, are you?' Ella said she might with some of them if she could get enough sugar. 'Could perhaps let you have some in exchange for a jar or two of the jam, eh?' People like Mrs Sadler-Browne had ways and means of getting the little extras that others had to do without. 'How's your father? I don't seem to have seen much of him lately.'

'He's not been too well.'

'No. He didn't look well the last time I talked to him.

Worried about the war, I gathered. I'm not surprised. Those that aren't worried now never will be. We're in a mess.'

'You don't think we might lose, do you?' Ella ventured.

She did not know whether to believe half of what she read in the papers or heard on the wireless. They had tried to make out that Dunkirk was a great victory. Some folk had said they only needed a few more such victories and there would be nothing to defend. But Mrs Sadler-Browne brushed aside such doubt.

'Lose? We shan't *lose*. Those fighter lads are working wonders, shooting down Gerries faster than I can shoot birds. But we've a long way to go before we win. The sooner the Americans come in the better. Then we can get on with it. I can't understand why they're shilly-shallying. Heard from your husband yet?'

For a second Ella wondered if Mrs Sadler-Browne thought that Walter might be privy to inside information from the other side of the Atlantic. She said she had heard, and that Walter was settling in and enjoying the country and the work.

'Canada's a fine country,' Mrs Sadler-Browne said. 'I was there myself once. Rather fancied settling and doing some farming. I hadn't got a husband then, though. Now I've got one that roams the world collecting flowers and can't stop long enough in one place to plant any.' She gave a short barking laugh.

Ella was mildly curious about Mr Browne and, indeed, about Mildred Sadler-Browne's marriage. Was it one of what they called 'convenience' rather than a love match, and if so, what were its advantages? She wondered if it included a sex-life, or if Mrs Sadler-Browne pushed him off and told him she could not be bothered with all that stuff and nonsense. She was not a bad-looking woman when she took a bit of care, but she was so mannish in her ways Ella found it impossible to imagine her submitting to a man, leave aside letting herself go as she had once or twice with Walter.

129

'It can't be easy to travel about, the way things are just now.'

'He's in the Far East,' Mrs Sadler-Browne told her. 'I had a letter from Borneo the other day. He says he's coming home to do his bit. I can't imagine what that might turn out to be. One of the Ministries, perhaps. Hush-hush stuff. The Germans have been working on biological warfare. Did you know that? Suppose they could drop chemical bombs that could kill all our crops and grass? We'd be in a sorry plight then, wouldn't we?' She narrowed her eyes to focus on something behind Ella. 'Does that chap think he knows one of us?'

As Ella turned to look the soldier was already moving on along the public footpath. All she could make out was a blur of khaki between the slats of the fence.

'Taking all in,' Mrs Sadler-Browne said. 'Perhaps he recognises me from the canteen.'

She was a mainstay of the local WVS and supervised the running of a canteen for servicemen in the Sunday-school-room of one of the chapels. Soldiers had started coming into the town early in the year and their number had increased after Dunkirk. They were billeted in the converted warehouse of one of the mills, units in the constantly shifting patterns of wartime duty, uprooted from homes, families, jobs; under orders for the duration; some of them already blooded, others who had yet to hear an enemy shot. Ella knew none of their faces. They were knots of khaki on street corners, khaki rows in the pictures, occasional columns marching, unarmed, at ease, from one place to another. Unattached girls were drawn to where they were; sometimes seen arm-in-arm, sometimes scandalously closer still in the darkness of shop doorways. Married Ella let them alone, while the censorious and the prurient waited for the first crop of pregnancies.

'Mildred Sadler's been asking about you,' she told her father when she went into the house.

'Was that her gun I heard?'

'She shot a pigeon. Nearly frightened me out of me wits.'

'She'll shoot owt 'at moves on her side of that wall.'

Sugden had his glasses on and was poring over last night's paper. Sometimes, thwarted by too many difficult sentences, he had not finished when the new one came; but bits that he could fathom and which he thought would interest her, he read slowly aloud to Patience. It was Ella's task, each evening after tea, to scan the fresh paper and summarise its most important contents.

Ella was worried about her father. He seemed to her to have aged too suddenly, and he had lost weight. You could see that in the way the flesh had fallen under his cheekbones and in his hands. He tired more easily. He spent less time in his garden and when he was there she had seen him standing looking aimlessly about, as if undecided what to do next.

'Have you changed them library books yet?' he wanted to know now.

'I'm going as soon as I've washed and changed.'

It was Saturday. Ella had worked the half-shift at the mill. Normally, at this time, Sugden would get up and go out for a while, giving Ella privacy; but now he simply moved his chair so that its back was square to the sink as she poured hot water from kettle to bowl, took off her blouse and slipped the straps of her camisole off her shoulders. She covered herself again before going upstairs to put on fresh clothes.

Lately, she had been reading to her parents each evening. It had come about one night when, breaking into her private absorption, Sugden had said, 'It seems to be holdin' you spellbound, that book, Ella. Is it owt 'at 'ud interest your mam'n me?'

'I don't know.'

'Has it a good tale, I mean? Is it a blood and thunder or a love book?'

'There's summat of all sorts in it.'

'Why doesn't tha' read us a bit, then?'

131

'Aloud, you mean?'

'We shan't hear it if it's not aloud, lass.'

She had been self-conscious at first, but she had soon trained her delivery from a sing-song to something more natural; though she often stumbled and lost the sense by having to breathe in the wrong place, mispronounced some words, and had to stop to look up others in the dictionary. It meant also, of course, that she now had to choose books less haphazardly than before, trying to please Sugden and Patience as well as herself, and looking through them with more care in case there were any embarrassing bits. It was one thing reading an embarrassing bit to yourself, another altogether coming across one while you were reading aloud.

# Ten

There was hardly anybody in the streets as she walked up through the town. Most of the shop windows had their blinds pulled. The front doors of a couple of pubs stood open. In one of them the landlord, in a white apron, was watering the tub of geraniums by the steps. She caught the smell of beer from the cool dim interior as he looked up and nodded to her. 'Grand evening.'

'It is.'

The air was soft and warm; and unusually clear, too, with so many coal fires unlighted. Soon people would appear after their evening meal, to make the most of the remaining daylight and the fine weather. Some would stroll into the park or down by the river; others make a leisurely circuit of residential streets, stopping from time to time to peer at other people's houses and gardens. Men would be playing bowls on the green behind the Working Men's Club. You could sit and watch that at the same time as seeing, by turning your head, the last overs of a cricket match in the field below. Shortly after seven a queue would form outside the pictures.

The free library was in a big single-storey building of blackened stone beside the main road. The words *Knowledge is Power* were incised over the doors. You were allowed to take out one volume of fiction and two of non-fiction at a time. There was a reading-room on the left as you went in, with two long oak tables with magazines laid out on them, and high desks at which you stood to read the newspapers, which were held by flat brass straps down the middle. Ella glanced in through the

133

glass partition as she crossed the lobby to the book room. It was quiet. She could see a boy in a school cap, an old man with a long white scarf tied in a knot at his throat and a couple of soldiers. The soldiers sat at a table and the one facing her was pointing out something in a magazine to the one with his back to her, and grinning.

Ella handed her book over the desk, and the librarian, a grey-haired woman with eye-glasses and an enormous cushion of a bosom, said she was glad she had returned it on time as it was in demand. She asked if Ella would like her to suggest something, but Ella said perhaps later, when she had had a quiet look round. Taking her ticket, she went through the little gate to the shelves where she went first to look, as she usually did, for a novel in the *Whiteoaks* series which followed on from the last one they had read. Then, lucky or not, she would spend some time dipping into anything that took her fancy.

Stepping round the end of a bookcase, from H/I to J/K a little while later, she came upon Olive Sims, who started at her appearance and, snapping shut the book she was holding, shoved it back on the shelf.

'It's you, Ella,' she said then. 'You made me jump.'

'Jump?' Ella said. It struck her as a funny place for someone to make you jump. 'You must have been miles away.'

'I must have been.' Olive had this odd look on her face, as though she had been caught out in something.

'Which book was it, if it was that fascinating?' Ella could not identify for certain the one Olive had put back as though it had burnt her fingers.

Olive's face took on an expression now that Ella had seen before. It usually accompanied the subject of sex. Olive glanced towards the librarian's desk, but they were quite hidden from it behind the tall bookcase. 'It just fell open there,' Olive said. 'As though any number of people knew about it.'

'What?' Ella asked.

With another look over her shoulder Olive took down

134

the book. 'Look,' she said in a whisper. Then: 'Damn, I can't find it now.' The long fingers of her thin-skinned narrow hands turned the pages as the colour rose in her face. Olive had the most transparent skin of any woman Ella knew. 'Here, I've got it. There, read it for yourself.'

There were this man and woman in a room by themselves and he was undressing her while she sat on a sofa. Ella thought it must take place in the last war because the man was in uniform; or he was to begin with. She heard Olive's suppressed snigger and felt the gust of her warm breath.

'It's that bit about his boots,' Olive said. 'Him keeping his boots on.'

Ella flipped the pages. 'Is it all like that?'

'I haven't had time to look right through.'

'Why don't you take it out an' read it?'

'With *her* lookin' at me over her glasses?'

'Other people have. Look, it was out a month ago. She's probably not even read it.'

'I wonder nobody's told her about it.'

'Complained, you mean? *You* tell her, if you want to.'

'Me? Nay, I'm not a spoilsport.'

'Go on, then,' Ella said, 'take it out and read it. Then you can tell t'lasses at mill.' She handed the book to Olive.

'I'd never dare take it home,' Olive said. 'What if me mam found it?'

'Well, it's not one for reading out loud to *my* mam'n dad,' Ella admitted.

'I can't make out whether they *do* anything,' Olive said, still fingering the book.

'I expect that's left to your imagination.' And that, where sex was concerned, was something Olive had in plenty. Poor Olive: it was like a fever that gripped her, filling her with a kind of fascinated revulsion. Ella pitied any chap who tried it on with her: she would either devour him whole or claw his face for him.

Ella moved on. If she didn't find something soon the place would close before she had chosen.

'Any luck?' The librarian had appeared with an armful of books which she was replacing on the shelves.

'Not yet.'

'You're spoiled for choice. Here, try this. It might be just the thing.'

'*Jane Eyre?*'

'Just the thing for reading aloud. Yorkshire, too.'

'Is it old-fashioned?'

'It's a classic.'

'There's nothing in it to upset me mam'n dad, is there?'

'I wouldn't recommend it if there were.'

'No. Well . . .' For some reason Ella did not fancy it; but there was not much time left for finding anything else.

'All right.'

Olive followed her out. 'Wait on, Ella. I'll walk part way with you.' There were two patches of colour burning in her cheeks as she joined Ella in the lobby. 'I got it. Look.'

'You did right.'

'I'm sure she knew, though.'

'If she knows it's because she's read it herself, so how can she look down on anybody else?'

'But it's her job.'

'It's her job to chuck out stuff she thinks is a bit too much an' all, so she must have decided that's not as bad as all that.'

'I don't think *I*'d have allowed it, if I was her.'

Oh, dear. Poor mixed-up Olive.

'Look, love,' Ella said, 'do you like it or don't you?'

'How do *I* know?' Olive said.

Remembering Daisy Marriott's words to her, Ella uttered them with all the authority of an experienced married woman:

'If the Good Lord invented anything better, Olive, he kept if for himself.'

'Is that true, Ella? Honest?'

'Cross my heart.'

A shiver ran the length of Olive's body. At the sight of the turmoil the very thought of it aroused in her work-mate, Ella was about to add a warning of the danger of getting married solely for the opportunity of going to bed with a man, when she was diverted by Olive herself saying, 'Wasn't that somebody speaking to you?'

Ella was left with an impression of a man's resonant voice as the powerful spring closed the heavy door behind them.

'Me?' she said.

'He said "Miss Palmer." One of them soldiers.'

Only one person had ever called her Miss Palmer. She felt the chasm open in her stomach, the blood drain from her face. With no conscious decision, but as though impelled, she pushed against the door as someone pulled it open from the other side.

'Miss Palmer.' He held his khaki forage cap between his hands. As the second soldier came out of the reading-room, Ella realised that Mr Strickland was the one who had been sitting with his back to the lobby. 'And I never recognised him,' she thought wonderingly. 'I could have gone away without knowing.'

'What are you doing here?' was all she could think of to say. Olive had come back in behind her, too stupid, too newsy or too man-mad to allow her a moment of privacy. Ella Palmer knows a soldier!

'I'm stationed here.'

'Oh.'

The second soldier was shorter, darker. He had a cheeky face, as Ella had noted when she had seen him grinning. He spoke directly to Olive while Ella and Mr Strickland stood locked for the moment in silence.

'Got something good there, have you?' Without a by-your-leave he took the book from Olive's hands and glanced at the spine. 'Good writer, is she?'

Olive, her face blotched again with colour, kept her eyes down. They seemed to fix themselves on the gleaming toecaps of the man's boots. A giggle suddenly escaped her.

Shifting position so that he stood between Ella and them, Mr Strickland said, 'You're looking well.'

'Am I? Thank you.'

She couldn't say the same for him. His face looked drawn. He wore his uniform as though it belonged to someone else. Perhaps, she thought, they had had a job to fit him, him being so tall yet slim with it. And how spruce he had looked in his dark suit and white shirt. How could men fight, she wondered, when robbed of their pride by that awful baggy battledress? He should have been an officer and had his uniform made to measure. But . . .

'I thought of calling at the house,' he was saying now. 'Then . . .' He seemed to take it for granted that she'd know.

Ella suddenly remembered the soldier who Mildred Sadler-Browne had noticed peering through the fence.

'Were you round there this afternoon?'

'I came to have a look. I've been before, but I've never seen you.'

Mr Strickland's friend was making Olive laugh. The peal of her laughter rose into the high ceiling, violating the rule about silence posted on notices in each room. The librarian came out with her coat on, locking a door behind her.

'We're closing now.'

'Are you in a hurry?' Mr Strickland asked. 'I'd like to talk to you.'

'They're expecting me at home now.' She didn't know why the excuse came so readily. There was no reason why she could not steal another half an hour or so. Except that there was Olive and the other man. And all the world to see them once they left the shelter of the building.

'Could we meet somewhere?'

Ella wondered where, how and, sadly, what for.

'I know what you must have been thinking about me,' he said when she did not reply.

But he didn't. And it was all too late.

'Mr Keighley died,' she said. 'Did you know?'

'No, I didn't.' He took it calmly, with no sign of regret, as if it were news of a stranger. Perhaps it seemed nothing now beside other deaths he'd known.

They followed Olive and the other man on to the steps.

'It's a lovely evening.'

'We deserve it after that terrible winter.'

'If only we got everything we deserved,' Mr Strickland said, 'and nothing we didn't.'

But who was to be the judge of that?

'Will you be stopping here long?'

'I don't know. All we hear is rumour. They could move us any time.' She stood silent. People walked by, turning their heads to look at another couple of local women being picked up by soldiers. 'Couldn't you come for a walk with me now?' he asked her.

'I can't.' She daren't: that was the truth of it.

'Can you spare me an hour one evening?'

'I don't know.'

'All I'm asking,' he said, 'is to see you just the once so that we can talk. You can make up your own mind whether to see me again after that.'

But could she? Was her mind her own to make up now?

'I don't know when to say,' she said. 'It's awkward. I'm working shifts.'

'Look, then . . .' He dragged a little red-backed note-book out of the top pocket of his battledress blouse and found a piece of pencil. It was a copying pencil: he licked the point before writing. 'Here's my number and where I can be found. Leave a message at the gate and it'll get to me. You will let me know something, won't you? It's very important to me.'

'I'll see. I can't promise, but I'll see.'

Ella slipped the folded scrap of paper into the opening of her cotton glove, already thinking of a safer place to hide it before she got home: the glove, sign of pride in her dress, which all through their conversation had hidden

Walter's ring. Why hadn't she told him? He would have to know if she saw him again and she acknowledged to herself now that she would not rest until she did see him. But was she playing fair in wanting to know what he might say before his awareness of her marriage could colour or curb it? No, she was not. 'You're a deceitful dolly, Ella Palmer,' she told herself, 'and it will do you no good.' She should have sent Mr Strickland on his way with no encouragement at all. Hadn't he a cheek, coming straight up to her like that? And hanging about the house, too. Had people where he came from no shame when they did the kind of thing he'd done? But it was only fear of being talked about and the need to think that made her leave him now.

'I'm going, Olive,' she called.

Olive, her hand to her mouth, was giggling again.

'Don't leave it too long,' Mr Strickland said.

Ella managed a little smile that he could read as he liked, and began to stroll away.

Olive caught her up. 'Wait on, Ella.'

'I thought you were there for the duration.'

'A pity he won't be.'

'Have you clicked, then?'

'He's asked me out, anyway.'

'He doesn't waste much time, does he?'

'No, he's not backward at coming forward.'

'Are you going?'

' 'Course I am. Why, don't you think I ought to?'

'That's up to you.'

'What d'you think's wrong with it?'

'You don't know him from Adam.'

'It's not Adam I'm going out with.'

'I wouldn't be too sure about that.'

'What are you gettin' so mouldy about – 'cos you can't make it a double date?'

'What do I want a soldier for? I've got a husband.'

'Does he know that?'

'Who?'

'Tony's mate.'

140

'Oh, you did get to know his name, then?'

'Why didn't he know yours? He called you Miss Palmer.'

'He's got good manners.'

'Why didn't he call you Mrs Lindley, then?'

'I knew him before the war. He didn't know I'd got married since.'

'You told him, o' course?'

' 'Course, I did.'

'If you're lying I can get to know, you know.'

'Why should I lie?'

'I don't know. I don't know why you want to be so mouldy, either. A mouldy spoilsport. Just because I've got a date with a chap and yours is on the other side of the world.'

Olive was right. And it was stupid of her to upset her, now of all times. For though Ella would have considered Olive one of the last people to be taken into her confidence, she could see no possibility of meeting Mr Strickland again without her help.

They paused on the corner where Olive would leave her.

'I'm sorry, Olive,' Ella said, 'but it was a bit of a shock seeing Mr Strickland again.'

'Mr Strickland?'

'Howard, his name is.'

'Oh, I like that,' Olive said. 'It's nearly as nice as Tony.'

'I don't want you to breathe a word of this to anybody else.'

'What?'

'What I'm goin' to tell you.'

'No, 'course not.'

'Promise faithful.'

'I promise.'

Olive's eyes were popping. Who would have believed it would turn into such an exciting evening – getting a date with a soldier and now hearing Ella Palmer's secrets? With the hollow feeling in the pit of her stomach that she was making a terrible mistake, Ella nevertheless took a deep breath and went on:

'Well, it's like this. Mr Strickland – Howard – came visiting on business a couple of years ago and I got the impression he took a fancy to me. He never said anything, mind, but that's what I thought.'

'I should say he still fancies you.'

'Well, I'm married now.'

'What went wrong? Didn't you fancy him?'

'It never had a chance to come to anything because he changed his job and the war came and we lost touch.'

'And you went and wed Walter Lindley. Oh, Ella, what a shame you didn't wait!'

'What's wrong with Walter, I'd like to know?'

'Nothing, Ella. I'm not saying anything against him. All the same, you didn't know Howard was going to turn up again, did you?'

'If you think I'm going to start any hanky-panky with him, Olive Sims . . .'

'I'm not saying you are. I wish you wouldn't be so touchy, Ella. What do you want *me* to do about it, anyway?'

'I want you to help me to see him again.'

'But you just said –'

'I know what I just said, but, you see . . . Well, I *didn't* tell him I was married.'

'Oh, Ella, everybody knows you are.'

'Well, I couldn't bring meself to tell him straight out. I want to break it gently, like. And I'd like to know what's happened to him since I saw him last.'

'I don't know what you're making such a secret of it all for. Invite him to his tea and tell him and have done with it. Do you want me to tell Tony to tell him?'

'No, I don't.'

Oh, lord, she wished she hadn't started all this. One trouble was, she didn't think it her place to tell Olive how Mr Strickland had disgraced himself, and why, for that reason, she could not tell her parents she had seen him. Unless, of course, that was the end of it and she had no intention of seeing him again.

'Y'see,' she said, 'me mam'n dad never took to him. Somebody told 'em summat about him that wasn't true. And in any case, they wanted me to marry Walter.'

'Your name 'ud be mud in two minutes if anybody saw you out with him,' Olive said.

'I know that, Olive. That's the trouble.'

'I think you're best off leavin' it alone.'

'You don't think women ought to make sacrifices in wartime, then?' Ella asked, and marvelled at her own duplicity.

'What sort o' sacrifices?'

'I mean do all we can for the lads who are fighting for us.'

'It depends what you mean by "all".'

'Who knows where Howard might be sent to from here? Who knows what danger he might be in?'

'Give up, Ella. I've only just met Tony.'

'Well, all I know is I'd never forgive meself if anything happened to Howard and I didn't feel I'd played fair with him.'

Olive frowned as she wrestled with the thought. 'Yes, I see what you mean. I mean, even if you are married, another chap what might have asked you has a right to . . . well, to some consideration.'

They nodded in unison. It was all that, for the moment, Ella could manage in response. For the phrases she had invented to soften up Olive had come so readily, she realised now, because they expressed what she really felt. And it was fear that thickened her throat now and robbed her of her voice. Who did know what might happen to Howard, to Walter, to any one of them?

But the obstacles in the way of a secret meeting daunted her. The network of her relatives, friends, workmates spread throughout the town and beyond. How could she get Mr Strickland's co-operation in trying to ensure they were not seen together, without telling him why it was imperative that they weren't? She had never felt so constrained by the small society she lived in; and that, she told herself, was because she had never before wished to do something she did not want others to know about.

'Send him a note,' she bade herself at one point. 'Tell him you're married and have done with it.'

And what then? How could she carry on as if nothing had happened while she knew he was in the town: knew he was there until one day she realised he was no longer there, that he had been posted out and was lost forever in the ebb and flow, the great tides of men that the war had put into motion? She could think of nothing to be gained by renewing their acquaintance, yet to let him go like that would be to root the few unsatisfactory minutes of their new meeting deep in her memory, to tantalise her for ever more.

She had trapped herself. She could no longer expect people to trust her to do what she thought best: there was a code of conduct laid down for her; things a respectable married woman did not do. And all this over a convicted thief! Behind his charm and his gentlemanly ways, Mr Strickland was capable of taking what was not his. While Walter, for all his rough edges, was as honest as the day was long; faithful, loving, reliable; steady as a rock.

The soft gaslight fell on the opening pages of *Jane Eyre*. They had lit the mantle early because Sugden and Patience were eager to hear Ella read from the new book. But, her thoughts in a turmoil, she stumbled so badly that Patience finally said she should leave it for today. They went to bed early and were early risers, and it was nearly time.

'You don't think you might be needing glasses, Ella?'

'No, my eyes are all right.'

'Have you something on your mind, then?' her mother asked.

'No, nothing special.'

Now was the moment to tell them: 'I met Mr Strickland today. I'm going to see him one more time because he could leave any day. I know what you think about him, but he's never had a chance to tell us his own tale. So I'm going to see him and if anybody tells you they've seen me with him you can tell them to mind their own business, because you know all about it.'

Straight out. Open. Above board. So what stopped her? What kept the words locked inside, unspoken, as Patience pottered about tidying and Sugden knocked the dottle from his pipe and took his watch from its hook to wind it. What had stopped her, she thought as she sat on alone a little while later, was that those words were less than the truth; that there was missing from them something which her father and mother in their sturdy everyday wisdom would have unerringly divined. She was in love with Mr Strickland. She always had been. And the thought of doing with him what she had learned to take pleasure in doing with Walter turned her faint with longing and fired her skin from head to toe with guilt at the treachery of her imagination.

Once she had acknowledged it she was overwhelmed. Her life seemed all at once pitched into chaos. Oh, she might summon the strength to put a face on things; but she saw nothing but a future of pretence and hopeless yearning. She had dreamed, as many girls did, of one day meeting a man who would fill her every waking thought; but she had not realised how bitterly mistimed it could be. So she felt cheated. She was still so young, so much at the beginning of everything, too inexperienced in the intimate life to lean instinctively on the compromise of the facts and shrug off the impossible. She could only rail at having cheated herself, at having been led into doing so by the people around her and the way they lived.

But she loved Walter, too. Or did she? She had taken a risk, but she liked and respected Walter and had not been repelled by the intimacy that marriage – any marriage worth the name – involved. And so the fact of her marriage, the sanctification of it, had begun to draw to itself the disguises of love and lay the foundation for its growth. But would the knowledge that she would never

145

see Walter again have brought the same feeling of unutterable dismay with which she now contemplated the everlasting loss of Howard Strickland?

The faint hiss of gas in the mantle hung on the silences between the rhythmic creak of her chair's rockers. To and fro, she rocked; to and fro, to and fro, until the small, deliberate sounds of her parents' movements ceased as they settled into bed. Then it seemed to Ella for a moment that she actually said out loud into the quiet the thought which hammered in her brain: 'I'm too young. How can I know these things?' And who was there to ask?

# Eleven

Spitfire Summer was what some people came to call it. Vapour trails entwined in cloudless skies as the boys in blue shot down German bombers in the almost unbelievable numbers that everybody was ready to believe because, like the gorgeous weather after that terrible winter, their victories put new heart into a people cast down by the setbacks of the spring and the fear of invasion. Why Hitler did not invade while the British army was still reeling after Dunkirk and the fall of France would be argued down to the present day. But he didn't, and as visions of a twentieth-century armada and skies filled with parachutes faded, the whole country seemed to heave a collective sigh of relief.

The long light evenings brought freedom from the frustrations of the blackout. People walked more jauntily; their faces relaxed as they smiled and joked. Always a new joke, always another rumour: 'They say that . . .', 'I hear that . . .', 'Have you heard the latest?'

'I hear Ella Palmer's thick with a soldier.'

'Ella? Never! She's got a husband abroad wi' t'RAF.'

'When t'cat's away . . .'

'Not Ella Palmer.'

'She's not t'first an' she won't be t'last.'

Ella wished the blacked-out nights were still here, if only for a while. Just long enough for her to meet Howard Strickland without being seen.

'It's easy,' Olive said. 'There's nowt to it.'

'How d'you make that out?'

On edge that Olive might blurt something out in front

of the other women, Ella had let herself be taken aside on the river bank where people were sunning themselves during their mid-day break.

'I'm goin' to t'pictures down town on Saturday night with Tony. He says Howard says will you come an' make it a double date.'

'A double date.' It was the language of American films: of girls in white-painted houses waiting for boys to drive up in open-topped motor cars and take them to college dances. They would have to queue. Ella knew they would have to queue. There were always queues at weekends at the town cinemas. They might have to stand outside in broad daylight for half an hour or more.

'What are you going to see?' she asked helplessly.

'What's it matter what we're going to see?' Olive said. 'You're going to see *him*, aren't you?'

'I don't know, Olive. I mean, I don't know if I should. If I can.'

' 'Course you can.' Olive nudged her. 'You can tell your mam'n dad you're goin' with me.'

Ella looked over her shoulder, thinking that this new intimacy with Olive was in itself likely to arouse curiosity.

'Olive Sims?' her mother said. 'I allus thought you didn't care for Olive Sims.'

'Oh, she's got her good points and she'll be company. I can't stop in for ever,' she added in a moment. She was tempted then to take it dangerously close to the truth by saying that Olive had got off with a soldier and wanted Ella to chaperone her on her first date. But it was safer to leave any thought of soldiers out of Patience's mind. It was obvious enough that Ella was brooding: she fell into long silences, sometimes failed to respond the first time she was spoken to, and forgot to do things in a way not at all like her.

'Are you worried about Walter?'

Ella was almost too straightforward to seize on that ready-made excuse:

'He's safe enough where he is, I suppose. All the same...'

She read Walter's letters to them, anyway; or the parts she did not mind sharing. He had been surprisingly bold once or twice, remembering how yielding she had become just before he had to go away, and making no bones about missing that; nor, it seemed, minding giving entertainment to the censor, whose occasional obliteration of a militarily sensitive line Ella would blame for her piecemeal offering of Walter's news. 'There's a bit blotted out,' she would say, when she could not find a ready paraphrase. Reading between the lines herself, she gathered that the training, though absorbing, was stretching him to his limit. What he did praise openly was Canadian hospitality and the plentiful food, commiserating with her on her having to put up with shortages and rationing. 'We'll never have it as good again,' he wrote, 'so we'd better enjoy it while we're here.'

And Patience, having had to discard the most satisfying and natural explanation of Ella's mood – that she was pregnant – accepted that she was missing Walter and the married state she had just got used to, while keeping a watchful eye open for signs of something else. All this Ella's guilty conscience made her acutely aware of.

Ella liked an occasional visit to the cinemas down town. They were bigger and got the best pictures before the local, showing them for a week in continuous performance from one o'clock each afternoon except Sunday; the only drawback with that arrangement being the difficulty in timing your arrival so that if you had to queue you didn't find yourself going in the middle of the main feature and seeing the end before the beginning. Inside, they all differed slightly in size, shape and style of decoration. Ella's favourite was the Embassy; not as big as the Ritz or the Rialto, but beautifully done out with bronze-coloured upholstery and a gathered curtain of satin-like sheen on which the lights slowly changed colour through soft washes of yellow, green, rose and purple as the theatre organ came up out of the floor to provide interval entertainment. Apart from dances, they were the most glamorous places Ella ever went to and she liked to look her best. To go to the local pictures she would sometimes just pop a coat over whatever she happened to be wearing; but for trips down town she always took special care. So there had been nothing out of the ordinary to cause comment in her preparations for her night out with Olive.

Now, with the house lights up and Howard gone for a moment to buy ice creams, Ella looked carefully round the packed circle to see if there was anybody she knew, and thought that while sitting on the back row would make things look all the worse if anyone did see her, at least she could be sure she was not being observed from behind. In the next seat, on her right, Olive turned her face and asked, 'How're you doing?'

'All right.' It was as long a sentence as she had uttered since getting off the bus. The sight of the two khaki-clad figures waiting in the entrance of the Market Arcade had brought her heart into her throat so that she could hardly breathe, let alone speak. And there had been no need to talk in the queue, for Tony held the stage, switching from one subject to another with hardly a pause, while Olive giggled and Howard looked at Ella until her face burned and she found herself glancing about for some way of standing apart, of seeming not to be with them, should she chance to spot someone she knew. 'These two soldiers got talking to us in the queue,' she could hear herself babbling. 'There was nothing we could do about it.' A bit of a romancer, that Tony, Ella was twigging. Telling them and everybody near how he'd met Robert Donat in a pub in London and spent the evening in his company. Ella hoped that Olive was not going to come a cropper over him; that she was capable of enjoying it for what it was worth and neither going too far nor expecting too much. Just at present it looked as if she was diving in headlong, for they had hardly been settled in the dark ten minutes before her arms were

150

wrapped round Tony and her mouth glued to his as though they would have to be prised apart. Ella sat primly through all that, her hands clasped lightly round the purse in her lap, while wondering how she would deal with any similar move on Howard's part. But he was not that kind of fast worker, as she had instinctively known. He simply sat quietly beside her, his elbow resting on the arm of his seat, apparently absorbed in the film except for those moments when he turned his head and she felt his gaze on her. What a ridiculous situation she had walked into! They could spend all evening together and say none of the things that needed to be said.

He came back with the ice creams. Ella handed tubs along to Olive and Tony, and opened her own as the man at the organ played a medley of the latest popular songs:

*Imagination, it's funny*
*It makes a cloudy day sunny*
*It makes a bee think of honey*
*Just as I think of you . . .*

And another one which Olive thought appropriate enough to sing a line from as she nudged Ella with the familiarity that sharing Ella's secret had given her: *I'm stepping out with a memory tonight . . .*

Olive said something that Ella did not catch. 'What?'
'Tony wants to go to a dance after.'
'Oh, yes?'
'What d'you say?'
'I can't go.'
'I'm going.'
'There's nobody stopping you.'
'Don't you mind if we split up?'
'I shan't have to, shall I?'
She had not yet faced the problem of getting home. It would still be light and there was bound to be someone of her acquaintance on the last buses. How could she get Howard by himself, clear up all this misunderstanding,

151

then go home alone with her reputation intact? As the lights dimmed for the main feature she thought of Walter's latest letter, come that morning, and felt once more in her stomach that yawning pit of fear and dismay. 'The work is hard,' Walter had written, 'and there is not much time to think about anything else. In one way I count that a blessing, because when I have a quiet few minutes I think only of you and all you gave me since our marriage. I shall never be able to thank you enough for all that, Ella my dear love, but when this lot is over I intend to spend the rest of my life being a good husband to you as you have been a wonderful wife to me . . .'

Heat broke in her and rose through her body to flood her throat and face with the force of a menopausal flush. Hardly aware of what she was doing, she stirred in her seat and peeled the cotton gloves off her sweating palms, something in her movements alerting the man beside her so that he turned his head and asked in a low voice, 'Are you all right?' Before she could collect herself his right hand had come over to rest on her left. She felt then his fingers find her ring, hesitate before testing its shape and precise location, and withdraw.

Several seconds passed before Ella could bring herself to look at him. He sat perfectly still, staring straight ahead at the movement on the screen. The soundtrack suddenly exploded with the clatter of machine-gun fire, the crash of breaking glass and the whine of a police car's siren; and as Howard bent his head and lifted his hand to his brow, Ella got up in a convulsive movement, and muttering, 'I shall have to go out,' began to stumble along the row, so quickly that nobody had time to stand for her and she worked her hands along the backs of the seats in front as sprawling legs impeded her flight.

An usherette sitting there glanced up from her task of threading ticket stubs on to a length of cotton with a needle on the end of it as Ella came out on to the carpeted semi-circular landing and walked to the rail overlooking the foyer. She felt the cooler air begin to chill the sticky heat of her armpits. The door opened again behind her. 'Ella . . .' Howard stood beside her.

Close to tears, Ella said, 'I'm sorry, I'm sorry. I should have told you straight away.'

For a moment he contemplated her while she hung her head. She had winded him, she knew. Everything must have changed for him in that few seconds while their hands touched; the only time they had touched in that way; the last time they ever could.

But now he took her elbow and turned her towards the stairs. 'Come on.'

'Where to?' she managed.

'You don't want to go back in, do you?'

'No.'

'Come on, then.'

She let herself be led down to the foyer and out through the glass doors. No one waited now. The last show was in progress. The street was still in the evening sun. Such weather! Across the road empty market stalls stood under the glass and iron canopy. A man moved between them, sweeping up the debris of the day's trading. They crossed over and strolled along one of the aisles.

'How long have you been married?'

'Three and a half months.'

'Where is he? In the forces?'

'The RAF. In Canada.'

'Is he a local man?'

'Yes. I've known him for years.'

'Was it a love match?'

What curious expressions he came out with! He was like no other man she had ever known in the things he said. When she did not answer, he said:

'Are you happy with him?'

She did not think he should have asked that, either.

'I'm only wondering what made you come tonight,' he said when she still hadn't spoken. 'Weren't you afraid you might be seen?'

'Terrified.'

'How long did you intend to keep me in the dark?'

'I wanted to see what you had to say.'

'Before you told me?'

'I couldn't believe it when I heard.'

'Couldn't you? Well, it's immaterial now.'

'Is it?'

They were about to emerge into the open air again. He stopped and perched on the edge of one of the stalls. Now his face was on a level with hers. He shook his head.

'No. I still value your good opinion.' He looked at her intently, then back down at the cap which he held between both hands. She watched his fingers folding it, touching the badge. 'Lots of people make one mistake, pay for it, then start afresh,' he said. He sat up, straightening his long back. 'But I didn't do it. That's what I'd say if I had done it – that I'd made one stupid mistake – but I didn't. I can't prove it. I'll never be able to prove it. But *I* know.'

'Was it somebody else, then?'

He shrugged. 'I can't prove that, either.'

'But if you didn't do it, somebody else must have.'

'Oh, yes.'

'To think you could go to prison for something somebody else did.'

'I expect it's happened before.'

'It doesn't bear thinking about.'

'That and many more things. Such as thinking that if only I'd got back here a year ago, say, you might not have married the chap you did marry.' He squinted up at her. 'Have I got any reason to believe that?'

'Don't plague yourself with what can't be altered, Howard.'

It was the first time he had heard her speak his given name. It brought his gaze back to her face again.

'Is that what you wanted to hear me say before you told me?'

'That wouldn't have been fair, would it?' Oh, no, it wouldn't; but it was what she had wanted. 'I just couldn't bring meself to tell you straight out. I thought if I did we wouldn't see each other again and I'd never get to know about . . . about the other thing.'

He said, 'Well, now you do know. Whether you believe me or not.'

'Isn't it obvious I do want to believe you?'

'You might want to; but why should you?'

'Because you've told me so.'

He looked as if he wanted to say something to that, but he just swallowed and went quiet.

The sun was going down on this side of the market building, so that although they were under the canopy they were not in its shadow. The man sweeping up had gone from their sight.

'Does he love you?'

'Yes.' She nearly added, 'He's mad about me.'

'You've got all you need, haven't you?'

'Apart from plenty of money, yes.'

'Will you tell your parents you've seen me?'

'I might say I bumped into you.'

'Will you tell them what I've told you?'

'Yes.' Not that she could guarantee they would believe it.

'I don't like the idea of them thinking badly of me.'

'If it had been anybody else who told 'em,' Ella said; 'but they thought the world of Mr Keighley.'

'You said he'd died?'

'Yes. Towards the back end of last year. His wife wrote to tell us. It sounded sudden.'

'Well, let him rest in peace, then.'

Ella did not know what he meant by that and found that she did not want to ask. The town-hall clock struck the hour two streets away. Ten o'clock.

'I ought to be going.'

'Home?'

'Yes.'

'Won't your friend be wondering about you?'

'No; she's got something else to think about.'

'I expect you'd prefer to ride back on your own.'

'It'll be safer.'

'Thanks for coming, anyway.'

She could not get her feet to take her away: that simple action would be so final.

'Have you still no idea when you might be going?'

'It can't be long now.'

'And I don't suppose you know where they'll send you?'

'No.'

She ached to touch him: to step forward and hold his head against her shoulder.

'I'll probably not see you again, then?' he said.

'It's better not.'

'Perhaps . . . if I got word to you when I knew we were going . . .'

'I expect Olive will tell me.'

'She seems quite taken with Tony.'

'Is he to be trusted?'

'In what way?'

'She hasn't had much experience.'

'Isn't she a sensible girl?'

'Not about that, perhaps.'

'Not like you, you mean.'

'She's not in my position.'

'I don't know much about him. You run up against all sorts in the army.'

'You mate up, though, don't you?'

'He's good company.'

'Perhaps you could drop him a hint.'

'Is she a good friend of yours?'

'No, but we work together and I know how she'd take it if he let her down.'

'What does she expect of him?'

'Only what she's a right to expect. That he'll play fair. That he won't lead her on if he doesn't mean it.'

He shrugged. 'If she throws herself at him . . .'

She was disappointed. She had expected more of him. It showed in the hardening of her voice as she said:

'You men, you see it all one way, don't you?'

Her colour was up. He saw it, and said with a matching

156

touch of impatience, 'Why are we spending what little time we've got left talking about them?'

'Because there's no point in talking about us,' Ella said, with a brutal directness that hurt her as much as she guessed it hurt him.

'This war,' he muttered. 'This bloody awful war.'

'Why didn't you write and explain before?'

'I don't know. I was ashamed and upset. I thought that somehow or other the truth might come out. Then . . . well, events took over.'

'And brought you back here again.'

'And too late.'

'We don't know anything about each other.'

'We might have been given a little while to find out.'

The sun, setting now behind the corner of a high, blackened building across the square, suddenly shafted straight into his face. He screwed up his eyes and shifted along the stall. I shall look back on this in years to come, Ella thought, like something I dreamed, something not real: the two of them lingering in the deserted market where only a few hours ago people had jostled and thronged; every word either of them spoke heightening the trance-like spell of what might have been. Why have I let it go so far? she asked herself. What was it had led him to think he could say all those things – something in her manner when they met at the library; her apparent readiness to see him again; her failure to tell him what he'd had a right to know from the start? Yes, she had given herself away, all right. But how long had he felt what he was telling her he felt now: telling her as plain as if he'd confessed it straight out? Ever since he'd stayed at the house or only when he found himself here again? He was soft, she told herself: not strong as she had once thought, but soft. His courteous way hid a sentimental nature that yearned most for what it could not have. And she had been no better herself. They were like two whining kids looking at sweets in a shop window, with money in their hands but unable to buy because the shop was shut.

So it was impatience with herself that led her to say now, with no effort to spare his feelings:

'This gets dafter by the minute.'

He would not look at her then. Instead, he got up and walked a few paces away from her. She spoke to his back: 'I've got to go now.' He did not answer. She raised her voice: 'I hope you'll be all right, wherever they do send you.'

He moved again, increasing the space between them. She took a couple of hesitant steps after him. Then, aware of the futility of it all and, as the town-hall clock struck the quarter-hour, of the immediate problem of catching her bus, she swung round and began to walk quickly towards the bus station.

As she got closer she saw a bus pull in which she knew would empty and turn round and take her the way she wanted to go. Not sure since the reshuffling of schedules whether or not it was the last, she broke into a trot. It was when she stepped off the pavement into the road to get past three people walking abreast that she stumbled and went down so far she had to put out a hand to save herself. There was a big stain of petrol and motor oil on the road there. It had separated into quite pretty rainbow colours, but what it left on Ella's cotton glove was black, foul-smelling and enough to make her cry.

# Twelve

Ella went to see Walter's father. Eddie Lindley was quite a bit younger than her parents, a man still in the prime of life, and she had wondered why he had not married again, though with Nellie two doors away he did not need another woman to do for him. Ella herself always liked to find a job when she was there, but the most she ever managed was to wash up the few things he had used for his solitary meal. 'Oh, our Nellie sees to all that,' he would say if she suggested anything else; and Ella did not want to risk offending her sister-in-law by taking too much on herself. So she mostly sat and stroked Eddie Lindley's long-haired mongrel bitch, Floss, which rested its head on her knee and gazed at her with soft, appealing eyes. Ella tried to pop round once a week; but they were duty calls. Though Eddie Lindley was amiable enough, she somehow could not warm to him.

He was of middle height, with a ruddy complexion and full, fleshy lips, like Walter's. But, unlike Walter's, his hair was dark and had receded to a straight line across the top of his head. As Ella's father had once said, he was hardly ever short of something to talk about, and he had a way of moving, sort of stiff-backed and turning on his heels, that made you guess he was opinionated before you heard him speak. It showed most on the cricket field. He was on the committee of the Working Men's Club and umpired their matches. You could tell he enjoyed that, standing there in his spotless white coat (another chore for Nellie), sometimes taking a couple of steps then turning on his heel, his face never slipping. 'He right fancies his sen' doin' that job,' Ella had once heard a spectator say. 'He's fair, though,' had come back from another man.

'You've heard from our Walter again, then?' Eddie Lindley would say when a letter had arrived. 'You'd better tell me what he's up to, 'cos he can't be bothered to write to me.' And Ella would give him the gist of it – all that concerned him – though she never took the letters themselves because she always had the feeling that Eddie would expect her to let him read them, and they were much too private for that. If she had timed her call well (so that she could say she had been but would not have to linger), Lindley would also say, 'I was just going out to the Club.' He went to the Club quite often, and when she thought of the intimacies of their married life which Walter alluded to in his letters, Ella had to smile as she remembered how he had tried to take advantage of the frequently empty house by inviting her there so that she might be persuaded to make love. But she had gone only a couple of times. Walter had never known when to stop, and Ella, even after she had agreed to marry him, had no intention of going all the way again until she had his ring on her finger. She had been right, too. It had been better for the waiting, quite apart from how it would have looked had Nellie, say, taken it into her head to pop round and found them upstairs, or up to something behind a locked door. When a man got worked up, a woman had to think for both of them.

Gelders Yard sloped down from the street. A dozen houses formed the other three sides of the square. Those across the bottom had four steps up to the door. The gaps left at the corners gave access to two blocks of w.c.s: one for every two families. The houses had two bedrooms, a living-room and a scullery-kitchen. There was a run of flagstones round the square in front of the houses; the rest of the yard was a rough surface of stones and trodden-down soil. Children sometimes played there, but the older ones had to go elsewhere with their ball-games for fear of broken windows. In warm weather there was nearly always someone sitting out, either on the step or on a chair brought down on to the flags. At number one an old ex-collier spent most of his time sitting in his open doorway, from where he could see everything that went on up the street: just sat and watched for hours on end. Well, you thought of him as old, though he was only sixty or so. He had had to come out of the pit because of dust in his lungs. His face was drip white and his breathing so laboured it was like taking painful bites out of the air. 'Turns your lungs to stone, that does,' Eddie Lindley had once said. 'They ought to show him to every young lad 'at fancies going down.' 'Somebody's got to get coal,' Ella had replied. 'There'll allus be enough of 'em to let the rest of us, with more sense, do summat else,' Lindley had given back, and Ella had gone quiet, turning over in her mind the implied slur on most of the men in her family. They grumbled constantly about the pit and the stinginess of the owners; yet they also tended to look down on anyone outside their trade as being afraid of real work.

Oh, they all worked hard, in their different ways, when there was work to go to; and saw little enough for it. Regular work had been the aim of all of them, before the war. No matter how poorly paid you were, within reason, if it was regular you could plan. Provided she wasn't saddled with a boozer or a gambler, but had a man who brought his money home, a woman could see that her family was clothed and fed, that the bills were paid, and perhaps a bit put aside for treats and holidays. A thrifty woman, that was; for there were some who never learned to manage and dragged their men down to their own hopeless level. You could pick out the ones who never let up and those who had already let go in even a tiny community like Gelders Yard; in the contrast between those houses with scrubbed and ruddled steps and clean lace curtains, and others whose privacy seemed to depend solely on the amount of grime accumulated on the windows. They stank, some of those houses.

When you were very young you did not choose your friends for the cleanliness of their homes (though sometimes your parents chose for you), and more than once, calling for a mate, Ella had stood on a step wanting to retch at the stench of a fetid, bug-ridden interior. But it never struck her then what impoverished conditions even the best of them endured: the spartan convenience of outside lavatories that froze in winter; every drop of hot water in the house to be heated on the fire; the reluctant coming to warmth of rooms in which the fire had to be rekindled each day; the bone numbing chill of every room except that where the fire burned, and the consequent huddling together of families in that one room, with privacy sacrificed to the need for warmth. She accepted it all because she had nothing to compare it with that was not outside her station. True, there were those new semis on the low side of town, one of which Walter had said he was determined to find a way of buying when the war was over. But Ella had not let her mind dwell on that possibility: there were too many things that could go wrong before then.

Walter's father was in the doorway shaking his tablecloth as Ella walked down the yard. She liked the pride that made him use a cloth when many a man on his own would have managed with a sheet of newspaper. Lindley had his Sunday dinner with Nellie and her family, but during the week she usually took something in for him. Ella did not blame him for preferring the tidiness of his own house. Nellie's kids were noisy and mischievous, and Les Farrar, her husband, quiet as an old sheep and easyful with it, often could not be bothered to get out of his mill clothes, which smelled of dyes and grease. Les was outside, kneeling beside his upturned push-bike, and gave Ella a shy little nod as she passed.

'Now then, Ella,' Eddie Lindley said when she had followed him into the house. 'What's new?'

'Nowt so much.'

'Well, that's soon talked about.'

Lindley put the folded tablecloth into a drawer of the sideboard and began to transfer cigarettes into a chrome-plated case from a packet of Capstan. He lit one with his petrol-lighter. He had a neat way of smoking, holding the cigarette lightly between his fingers and taking such slow appreciative drags Ella sometimes wished she smoked herself so that she could share his obvious enjoyment.

Floss came in from outside and walked towards her with tail wagging. Ella crouched and took the loose skin below the dog's ears in both hands. 'Hullo, girl. Who's a fussy body, then?'

'I had a letter from our Walter this morning,' Lindley said.

'Oh?'

'Aye. Wonders never cease.'

'He's got a lot to think about.'

'Oh aye, they seem to be keeping him busy.'

'Had he anything special to say?'

'Nowt you don't already know about, I don't expect. He doesn't seem to be missing home much.'

'Oh, but he does,' Ella said impulsively. 'He misses me.'

Lindley's gaze flickered over her as she straightened up.

'Well, that's different.' Ella pulled out a chair from the table and sat down. 'Funny to think we might end up with an officer in the family. We shall all have to mind our manners then.' He sounded to Ella as if he was jealous of his own son.

'All I can think about is that he's safe where he is.'

'Safely out o' t'road, you mean?'

'Out o' t'road o' t'fighting,' she said. What else could he have thought she meant?

'He won't stop in Canada for ever. They're not training him for that.'

She liked Walter's father none the more for reminding her. 'We'll think about that when he comes back,' she said.

'I reckon we'll soon be shut of some of these soldiers an' all.'

'Where did you hear that?'

'One of their officers came to t'Club to fix up a cricket match.'

'He'd never tell you what their plans were, did he?'

'No, but he asked for an early fixture.'

Lindley seemed to have officers on the brain; but if he thought that Walter was going to become one he might have another think coming. Ella read too much between the lines of Walter's letters to regard that as a certainty. As for the soldiers, everybody knew they couldn't stay long, without Lindley offering it as inside information. Was it what he was saying or her own mood that rubbed her up the wrong way today?

He was still talking: 'We'll be better off without 'em, if you ask me. All them fit young men hanging about in a place this size. Time on their hands. Chaps away from their homes and coming into contact with women who don't know any better and others with their own men away. It does nowt but breed bother.'

'Oh, you'll always get a bit of that.'

She was wondering where Lindley thought soldiers ought to be put to keep them away from the people they were supposed to be fighting for, when the shot she had feared came at her from this unexpected quarter. Or, in Lindley's own cricketing parlance, a deceptive ball was delivered and was on the bat before she could select a stroke.

'Have you run up against any of 'em yourself?'

'In what way?'

Was it good enough? Safer than a straight denial; more natural than a babbled explanation? The light was behind her. She hoped she was not going to colour up. She bowed her head as she reached down to fondle the dog.

'Haven't you had your walk today, then? Is that what you want?'

'Somebody said they thought they'd seen you being

pestered by a couple of 'em outside t'Embassy cinema the other Saturday night.'

It was that 'pestered' that restored some of Ella's composure.

'Oh, you mean me an' Olive Sims. You can't give 'em the cold shoulder altogether, can you? What would we think if somebody did it to one of ours?'

'They'll not need much encouragement, all t'same.'

'They seemed nice enough chaps.' Emboldened, she added, 'Olive went off to a dance with 'em. I came home on me own.'

'Is she single, this Olive?'

'Oh, yes. She can do as she likes.'

'A lot have thought they could.'

'I had a word with her afterwards and told her to be careful.'

She felt Lindley's gaze linger on her before he stirred and threw his cigarette end into the empty firegrate. The sound of children's voices came from the yard.

'That's our Nellie's two. Have you been in to see her?'

'No. I'll pop in for a minute, if you're going out.'

'I'll be having a walk down to t'Club when I've washed an' sided me few pots.'

'I can do that for you.'

'Nay, there's no need. It won't take five minutes.'

Ella got up and replaced her chair. 'Is there anything else I can do while I'm here?'

'Nowt 'at's spoiling.'

'I'll go round and have a word with Nellie, then.'

'Aye, you do. The bairns like to see you. They mustn't know you're here or they'd have been in.'

'They're a handful just now. Into everything.'

'It's only bairn-like,' Lindley said. 'They'll grow out of it soon enough.'

On an impulse to offer him something, Ella said, 'Walter and me's talked about a family, y'know.'

'Oh, yes?'

'We decided it'd be best left till we had a home of our own. We're both young enough to wait a while; but me

165

mam'n dad are past the age of dealing with young 'uns in the house.'

'You'll have to wait an' see what happens when he comes back from Canada. You can't allus plan these things. And our Walter's got a mind of his own. Allus had. When he gets set on summat there's no shifting him.'

'Oh, I know that.'

'He got you that road, didn't he?' Lindley said, with a directness that once more caught her off-balance. 'I thought at one time he wouldn't manage it.'

'You thought wrong, then, didn't you?'

'Evidently so. On t'other hand, there's more to marriage than four legs in a bed. Only time sorts that out.'

'I don't know 'at there's any call for talk like that.'

'Happen not,' he conceded, but with no hint of an apology. 'I'm just saying you can't put old heads on young shoulders.'

She wanted to flash at him then: 'Don't you trust me? Do you think your Walter's too good for me; or do you think I think I'm too good for *him*?' But her knowledge of her confused feelings held her back. Instead, she said, 'Well, like you say, only time'll sort that out.' And to let him see that he had offended her, she turned abruptly from him and stepped out into the evening sunlight.

Nellie's younger child threw himself at her as she reached the flags, and the exertion of scooping him up gave an understandable reason for her colour and the still-rapid beat of her heart.

'Auntie Ella! Auntie Ella!'

'Ooh, you are a rough young body. If you do that when you're much bigger you'll have me down.'

'Have you got any spice, Auntie Ella?'

'Is that all you want me for, then – spice?'

'I want some chocolate.'

'I haven't any chocolate. But I want a kiss.'

The boy rocked backwards and forwards in her arms, pushing at her shoulders with both hands.

'Give us some chocolate, Auntie Ella.'

'No chocolate, no kisses. Is that it? It's nowt but cupboard love and I thought we were friends.'

He flung his arms round her neck and brushed the saliva of his wet kisses on to her cheek.

'That's more like it. Now I know it's genuine. Let's see what there is in me pocket. Here, you can have a Yorkshire mixture; it'll last you longer than chocolate.' She popped the two-coloured boiled sweet in the shape of a fish into the waiting mouth. 'Suck it, don't chomp it. And mind you don't swallow it whole and choke yourself.'

Nellie appeared in the doorway with her other child clutching her skirt, as Ralph got down. The girl was less forward than her young brother, with more of her father's shy nature.

'Now then, Betsy, what have you got to say for yourself?'

'Say hullo to your Auntie Ella, Betsy.'

'Cat's got her tongue. I saw it runnin' up t'yard chewing summat.'

A smile broke across the child's face. She chuckled. 'It hasn't.'

'Hasn't it? Let's have a look, then.'

'Learnin' her to stick her tongue out,' Nellie said. 'She'll be doing it when she's not supposed to.'

'Pop it back in, then,' Ella said. She held out the bag. 'Would you like one of these?'

'Yes.'

'Yes what?' Nellie said.

'Yes, please.'

'That's right, love. Come on now and give your Auntie Ella a cuddle.' As the child let herself be lifted, Ella's hand cupped a plump half-moon of silky smooth flesh. 'Where are your knickers, Betsy?'

'She wet 'em,' Nellie said. 'I wa' just debatin' whether to put her another pair on or not bother before she goes to bed. Are you comin' in?'

'I'll have a minute.'

Short-boned, like her father and brother, Nellie had put on weight after the birth of her two children. It was, Ella thought, in keeping with her unruffled nature and easy going attitude to life. She moved some clothes off a chair so that Ella could sit down.

'There's no doubt about it, Ella: you'll have two or three of your own.'

'Oh, I've just been over all that with your dad.'

'Oh, have you?'

'I was telling him we'd decided to wait till we have a place of our own.'

'Well, there's nowt to make you change your mind while Walter's where he is.'

'No, and plenty of time to talk it over again when he comes back.'

'Les an' me have never talked about it yet,' Nellie said. 'It was just summat 'at happened.'

'As long as you've found out what it is 'at causes it,' Ella could not resist.

'Cheeky dolly!' Nellie said. But it tickled her. She laughed and her laughter grew the more she thought about it. 'By God!' she said eventually, 'you'd be all right if you waited for somebody to tell you.'

'You would an' all.' Ella felt in her pocket as she remembered. 'I found this length of ribbon when I was turning a drawer out. I thought you might like it for Betsy's hair.'

'Ooh, thanks, love. Sure you won't need it yourself?'

'No, that's a better use for it.'

'It'll save for her Sunday best. See what a bonny ribbon your Auntie Ella's brought you, Betsy.'

'Can I have it for me teddy.'

'No, you can't have it for your teddy. It's getting as scarce as gold,' she said to Ella. 'God knows what we shall be short of before this lot's over.'

'As long as it's nowt worse than a length o' ribbon,' Ella said. 'But it will be.'

'Did me dad say he'd heard from Walter?'

'Yes.'

Nellie became pensive. 'I was thinking about you before you came.'

'What were you thinking?'

'Oh, mainly what hard lines it is to get wed, then have to part from your husband.'

'I expected it.'

'Aye . . . and better you did get wed and had the pleasure of it afore he went.'

'What d'you think'll happen with your Les?'

'He'll register with his age group, then we can only wait and see.'

'Millwork's important; happen they'll never take him.'

'An older man can do his job,' Nellie said. 'Happen a woman, even, if it came to it.'

They both fell silent, reflecting upon the unforeseeable eventualities which had entered their once predictable lives. Then Nellie stirred and said: 'Did me dad ask you about them soldiers?'

'Soldiers?'

'Them two outside t'pictures.'

'Oh, them,' Ella said. 'Is it front-page news, or summat?'

'Nay, he just came home from t'Club and said this chap he'd been talking to said he thought it wa' you he'd seen.'

'Me and Olive Sims,' Ella said. 'They were two of our lads, Nellie, not flamin' Germans.'

She poised herself for the response which would tell her she had over-reacted. But Nellie suddenly was not attending to her. She had got up and moved towards the open door as her attention was diverted.

'There's some lads shouting summat in t'street.'

'They're just playing about.'

'Nay, they're not.'

Ella joined her in the doorway. Funny, she thought a little later, how some people had that uncanny instinct for recognising the something just out of the ordinary which signalled disaster. And always, she thought, there was at such times the moment before you knew, then that after which you could never again not know.

169

Lindley was standing at the top of the yard with Mr Dexter, the retired miner, on his feet beside him. A boy in a man's cap came running and Lindley stepped into the street and caught him by the arm and spoke to him. By this time both Ella and Nellie were halfway up the yard and heard plainly what the lad said.

'There's been an explosion at t'pit, mister. An explosion an' a fire.'

'Who's on afternoons?' Ella asked.

She rested her weight on both hands on the table and tried to steady her breathing as Sugden and Patience looked at her, uncomprehending. She had run all the way.

'Ey, Ella,' her mother said, 'who's after you, lass?'

So the news had not yet reached this quarter of the town.

'Which of our lot's working?' she said. 'Don't you know?'

Her flushed face and high, excited voice brought them to their feet, their eyes wary in the slow recognition of catastrophe. It was Patience who spoke again.

'You'd best tell us what's happened.'

'I don't know much. There's some lads come up into t'village shoutin' about an explosion and a fire.'

'Lord above have mercy,' Patience murmured.

Now they looked helplessly at one another. 'Don't we know?' Ella asked again. She hoped it was none of them. Afternoons was the least popular of the three shifts. Some men did not mind it because it let them tend their gardens or allotments in a morning; others hated it because the pubs had shut by the time they came up. Ella's brothers liked their pint of a night; but they could not always choose. There were five men to be concerned about: Ronald, Wilson, Thomas; and Ronald's two lads, James and Arthur.

'To t'best of my knowledge,' Sugden said, 'they're all on reg'lar days.'

'Our Ronald went on nights a while back,' Patience

170

said, 'but he come off because he couldn't get his sleep.'

'We can't be certain,' Ella said. 'I shall have to go an' see 'em all. There's nowt else for it.'

'Don't stop callin', though, will you?' Patience said. 'Come back an' tell us. We s'll never rest till we know.'

And perhaps not for a long time once they did, Ella thought.

There was a knock at the door. It opened before Ella could reach it. 'Can I come in?' It was Winnie. They looked at her.

'Have you heard?'

'Only just.'

'Is our Thomas at home?' Patience asked.

Winnie's loose mouth trembled and her eyes brimmed with tears. 'No. That's just it. He's down there, among it all.'

'I thought he wor on days,' Sugden said.

'He was . . .' Winnie gulped. 'There wa' this deputy he was allus across with. Allus on to him, your Thomas said.'

'You mean he changed shifts to get out of his road?' Sugden asked.

'No.' Winnie shook her head. She could hardly speak now. 'Thomas gobbed him.' The tears welled over. Thinking she might fall, Ella pulled out a chair and gently pushed Winnie down on to it.

'Gobbed him?' Sugden said. 'That's a sacking job.'

'I know. But they were shorthanded on afternoons. T'manager said he'd give him another chance if he'd go and help out there. He only swapped over a couple of days ago. Oh God, and I don't know if he's safe or not. I came to see if Ella 'ud go to t'pit with me.'

'Where are your bairns?' Patience wanted to know.

'With a neighbour.'

'You could have brought 'em here.'

'They don't know 'at owt's wrong yet. They'll be all right with Mrs Coxson.' She got up. 'I shall have to go. Will you come with me, Ella?'

'Aye, I'll come.'

171

Sugden bent for his boots. 'I'll follow you down at me own speed. You'll go faster than me.'

Patience said, 'Is there any more of ours down there, Winnie?'

'No, only Thomas.'

'Are you sure?'

'Yes. *He* wouldn't have been there either, but for me.'

'Nay,' Sugden said, 'it wasn't you 'at gobbed that deputy.'

'No, but Thomas wanted to pack it in and try for a job up top somewhere. He said he was sick of it. I knew it'd be the army if he came out of t'pit, so I talked him into going on the other shift. I persuaded him. I wish I never had. Oh God, I wish I never had.'


'How could you know?' Ella said over and over to her sobbing sister-in-law as they waited with the crowd in the premature dusk created by the powerful extra lamps illuminating the pit-yard. They waited as near to the pit-bank as they were allowed to go. There were not yet enough policemen to marshal such a number, and though the last thing any of them wanted was to impede the work of rescue, they could not help re-encroaching on the wide lane that officials appealed to them to keep clear through their midst; so that at the approach of every vehicle carrying rescue and fire-fighting equipment, and the ambulances which could as yet only stand and wait, they had to press back on their already close ranks. A woman from the nearer village, three-quarters of a mile up the lane, told them how her house had shaken and her ornaments danced in the shock wave of the explosion.

Beyond the shed of the lights stood slim trunks of silver birch. Long ago a space had been cleared in a wood for the getting of coal, and oak and ash and beech still flourished at a safe distance. But the silver birch crowded close and were destroyed in slender youth by the relentless spread of smouldering colliery waste.

The winding-wheels turned, then were still; spun,

then stopped. Those men who had been working out of reach of the explosion and were not needed below had already come up. The news they brought with them had passed through the crowd until it blurred into rumour. There were ten men trapped beyond a fire and a massive fall of roof. No communication with them was possible yet. There was warily hopeful talk of their finding their way into the interconnected workings of another mine and being hauled to the surface three miles away. Some said they knew for a fact there was a way through, but that no accurate plans existed to guide rescuers in their approach from the other side. Ella thought it could not be as simple as that. Weren't there always two shafts and another way out nowadays? Hadn't that precaution become obligatory after some terrible disasters years ago? The ill-feeling aroused by the rumour, though, came out in angry murmurs about the grabbing incompetence of the coal-owners, whose only thought was to work men for their profits, when a chauffeur-driven Rolls-Royce carrying two elderly men in dark suits and starched white collars nosed in through the gate. But the crowd was mostly hushed, stoical in its growing fear. When a woman finally lost control and started to shout that she had one son at the bottom of the sea and now another trapped here, she was quietened and comforted and led away.

Ella spotted her father standing with Ronald and Wilson. Sugden wore a cap and a muffler and carried a walking-stick. Ella's brothers had changed back into their pit-clothes. They moved towards the office and Sugden turned when Ella called to him, shaking his head curtly as he approached and she asked him if there was anything new to add to what was common knowledge. He stood with them, a little apart, watching the activity on the pit-bank. It was only when – and rarely now – she saw him among a number of people that Ella realised anew that he was not a tall man. She always somehow thought of him as a tall man. He was silent, watching. Once or twice he glanced down as he scraped

173

in the coal-dust with the end of his stick. In a long life since he had first gone to work underground at the age of twelve, a life spent alongside the possibility of disaster, this had the makings of the worst calamity he had ever directly known.

Winnie's arm was held in Ella's, her trembling body pulled in close. She was never very clean at the best of times, Winnie, and now her sweat had the added pungency of fear. It was as Ella, suddenly acutely aware of this, turned her head away and contemplated her father, that something more appalling than anything they had allowed themselves to imagine occurred.

The ground moved beneath their feet. People staggered. Some clutched at their neighbours. Ella saw a woman thrown on to her knees as the colossal thump and fading rumble of another explosion tore through the workings below. Smoke and coal-dust funnelled out of the mouth of the shaft and for a while totally hid the headgear. Soot and dust spread in a foul umbrella of waste which showered on to the awestruck upturned faces of the crowd. And in the moment they collected themselves, and full realisation of what had happened came to them, the people gave voice in one long, concerted and agonised 'O-o-oh!'

# Thirteen

It was the sight of Aunt Selina that broke Ella. She had managed to hold it back until she saw the old woman crossing the road from the bus-stop. She carried a walking-stick as well as a carpetbag, and as a car came into view she showed a nimbleness surprising in one of her age and weight. The funeral was starting from Thomas's parents' house and Ella had been round to see if there was anything she could do for Winnie.

'Aunt Selina.'

The old lady stopped and faced her. 'Ella.'

It was then that something gave in Ella. She who had managed calm in the presence of the widow's grief now let go. Her throat filled. She felt her eyes brim and her face begin to work.

'Oh, Auntie love.'

'Aye, lass, aye.'

Aunt Selina transferred her bag, then put her arm through Ella's and gripped her forearm.

'Is your mam expecting me?'

'She seemed to think you'd be sure to be here, all else permitting.'

'Your Uncle Ezra 'ud ha' been with me an' all, only his sciatica's very troublesome.'

Like Ella, Patience was the youngest of her family. She had had several sisters, and one of Ella's earliest memories was of her world being occasionally crammed with formidable but kindly aunts and great aunts. They had all come together only at very special times, in Ella's experience, such as funerals. For some of them had married men whose work took them to live elsewhere, and since Ella was small three or four had died, usually in their eighties. One of the most frightening to a small child, till you got to know her, had been Aunt Selina, imposing in her big features, a wall eye and a booming contralto voice which she found it impossible to moderate.

Of her father's relatives, Ella had seen very little. They were something of a queer lot, Patience had once said, and on marrying and leaving home Sugden had seemed to settle for an arrangement whereby he would not bother them if they did not bother him. Ella wondered if any children she might have would grow up knowing as little about Ronald and Wilson, Ada and Doris. Of Thomas they could now only ever know a name, added to those of Edward, David and John: the ones who had died before their time.

Aunt Selina was early; the hearse would not arrive for another hour. It was customary to let people see the corpse, the open coffin standing where they could approach and pay their last respects. Only when it was time to leave for church was the lid put into place and screwed down. Ella remembered, when very small, being led up to peer at the waxen features of a great-uncle and listening to those around saying how he had shed twenty years in the few days since his death. But this funeral and the others were burials without bodies, with empty coffins ballasted to give them weight. Selina and Patience, veterans of the rituals of bereavement, had both laid out the dead, and the prospect of walking behind a coffin without a corpse disturbed them as it did Sugden. 'Not to know just where t'lad is, Selina,' Patience said. 'Not to know 'at you've laid him safely to rest.' Because for all they knew, Ella had thought during one mad moment, Thomas could walk in in the middle of it and demand to know what they thought they were up to. 'Who knows he's dead?' Winnie had burst out at one point. 'How can they prove it?' But they didn't have to. And while they all sat in church and sang and prayed and listened to the parson talk about somebody he would not have recognised on the street, the faces of the ten bodies entombed far below would shed their years under the pitmuck in the dark, then begin their slow return to the dust.

'Did our Thomas treat that lass right?' Aunt Selina asked while they were still just the few of them in the house; and Ella wondered how wind of that had blown the twelve miles to her aunt's ear.

Patience, too down for pretence, asked, 'What difference does it make at a time like this?'

'Very little just now,' Selina conceded. 'But it might in how soon she settles to it.'

'And what about his own flesh and blood? How do they settle to it?'

'Like they've allus done, Patience lass. If they're of an age some go upstairs an' make another. Otherwise they learn to 'bide what they have to 'bide. It's t'chance you take when you bring 'm into t'world. Sorry place that it is, taken all round.'

Others began to arrive, tapping on the door before stepping inside. Once they had made their presence known, the men relieved congestion inside the house by going to stand in the yard in their dark suits and hard hats, conversing in a desultory way, offering cigarettes, giving one another lights. Indoors, the talk was mostly about Winnie and the children and how they would manage, the question of Winnie's ability occasionally coming close to being held up for direct scrutiny, then discreetly dropped. It was no time to be critical.

Winnie came, standing in the doorway for several seconds before anyone noticed her. She had left Linda and Brian with a neighbour. Neither of them was old enough to understand what had happened. 'Never' was an impossible word to bairns of three and four, and, if spared the funeral, it could be allowed to grow into their lives gradually that they would not see their father again. That was Winnie's idea, at any rate, though not everybody agreed with it.

Martha, Ella's sister-in-law, gave Winnie her straight chair near the door. Winnie sat with her eyes downcast and fiddled with her black cotton gloves. She had bought a little black hat. Ella noticed that the hem was loose on her grey herringbone coat – much too heavy for this warm weather – and thought, 'I could have put a stitch in that if I'd known.' She hesitated to draw attention to it now. But better that than having people comment outside. She had to move Ada to get to her sewing-basket. Ada, who looked as usual to be wearing new from head to foot, was casting disdainful glances at Winnie, who might have been a distant relative the way she had slipped in and was keeping on the fringe of it all. They were a disappointment, people who would not play their part. Winnie was the stricken widow and she ought to be making the most of it, as Ada would have done in her place, instead of cowering at the back like an interloper.

Ella crouched beside Winnie. 'Hold still a minute.'

'What's wrong?'

'Your hem's down.'

'It's right enough,' Winnie muttered.

'Nay, it's not. I'll just put a tack in it an' you can stitch it yourself properly later on.'

Not that she expected she would. She would make do with the tacking stitch until that gave.

'Isn't it nearly time we were off?' Winnie asked.

'They're due in ten minutes.'

'I shall be glad when it's over.'

'We all shall.'

'Do we all know how we're getting there?' Doris asked. She was on her own, her two young ones at school and her husband, Jack Walford, unable, so she said, to break his work.

'There's two motor cars coming beside t'hearse,' Patience answered, 'an' our Ada and Cyril can take a two'r three more with them. Your father an' me an' Winnie 'ull be going in t'first car with your Aunt Selina an' our Ella. T'rest of you can sort yourselves out as you've a mind.'

'Our Ella?' Doris exclaimed. 'I thought t'oldest took preference.'

'Well, you're not t'oldest, so it makes no matter to you.'

'Our Ella's not t'oldest, either. It's summat when t'youngest goes first.'

'I'm not bothered how I go,' Ella said, straightening from mending her sister-in-law's coat. 'I can walk at back for all I care.'

'Oh aye, you'll say that now,' Doris said. Her colour was up and her quickness to displeasure made Ella flare.

'What's up wi' you, Doris? Have you come looking for summat to fall out about? 'Cos you might ha' picked a fitter occasion.'

'I'm just watching you gettin' your own way, just because you're t'last one at home an' you can say what you like, with nobody to contradict you.'

Ella was taken aback. 'Well, I've never heard owt so –'

'Our Ella gets contradicted when she needs contradicting, like anybody else,' Patience broke in. 'You just watch your tongue, Doris, and remember what we're all here for.'

'I'm only saying what I think's right,' Doris insisted.

'I want Ella with me,' Winnie said firmly. 'And that's an end to it.'

But of course it wasn't. It was the beginning of the long estrangement between Ella and Doris, something she had never sought and whose reasons she never did fathom, wondering later, as she did then, at the strength of her sister's resentment.

Then in the ensuing moment of surly silence Wilson stepped in from the yard, taking off his hard hat which had impressed a red furrow into his forehead. His voice grated with sarcasm as he looked across the room at his oldest sister.

'By gow, Ada,' he said, 'thy Cyril knows a lot about pits an' gerrin' coal for a chap 'at's never been no deeper underground than your gaffer's wine cellar.'

179

Someone let go a nervous snigger as Ada shifted on her chair, her chin going up. She would not have been lost for a retort, Ella was sure, but before she could frame anything Winnie was galvanised into life, both hands making fists to beat the air.

'Coal-gettin'! The pit! It's all you lot can think about, gettin' coal and goin' down t'pit. It's all you're fit for – that an' fallin' out over nothing. That's why we're all here today. That's why *he*'s down yonder, where you took him an' left him. I could have got him out long since, but no, he had to be a man, like the rest of you. Bloody men. Bloody women an' all, 'at let 'em do what they like.'

# Fourteen

It was Ella who sat with Winnie when they had all gone
their ways and the children were settled for the night.

'Nobody knew him better than I did. Oh, I know you
were his sister and nearer to him in age than the others
and you were his favourite. You were, you know. He
might never have told you or showed much, but he said
to me many a time, "Our Ella's a lady." He used to say it
sometimes when I thought he was only trying to rile me,
telling me all I wasn't. I even think I shouted at him one
time, "It's a pity you couldn't have wed your Ella if she's
so bloody wonderful!" I did. Oh, I can tell you that now
because it was only when he'd driven me so far I hardly
knew what I was saying. I'd say anything then just to try
to get at him. Nothing personal, you understand, Ella.
Far from it. I've never had anything against you. But
nobody knew him better than I did. I knew it the minute I
laid eyes on him when he came into t'farmyard with his
two mates. I never looked at them: only him. He could
have brought two different lads altogether next time for
all I'd have known. But I knew I'd know him. Oh, yes.
And him me.

'They were after a drink o' tea. I thought at first 'at
they knew what I had in the can, 'cos I was just coming
back from taking the men their allowance. "Mornin'!" he
calls out, and the other two hung back till they saw I
wasn't going to bite him. "We was wonderin' if there
was any chance of a drink o' tea," and I thought here's a
bold 'un. He's one to be watched. But when he come closer
there was something else in his eyes 'at told me not to be

181

hasty. A shyness. He didn't like what he was doing. I thought he'd been egged on. But a defiance an' all, that for two pins would have taken that can from me and emptied what was left in it over the yard. Mebbe I didn't see all that in his look before I spoke, or mebbe I said what I said in spite of it.

' "Does it look like a cafe?"

'Now what did I want to say a thing like that for, I wonder?

' "I can't see owt else 'at looks like one," he says. "We'd just like to buy a jug o' tea, if you can oblige. We've got our own snap."

'I knew then what they were: colliers, out of work. It turned out they'd decided one day to ride the bus to the terminus. Just for a change of air, Thomas said.

'Well, I was only skivvying there. They could have had what was left in the can for me; but I didn't own the place.

' "I'll have to see what the missus says."

'I went in and told Mrs Atkinson and she came and looked round a lace curtain at them.

' "What d'you say they want – tea?"

' "Just a drink, to wash their bait down."

' "Do they expect cups and saucers as well?"

' "I shouldn't think so."

' "I heard somewhere that they drink out of jam-jars at home." She did. Gospel. That's what she said. I didn't argue with her. As far as I knew she could be right; but I didn't think so. I didn't think colliers were a race apart; just working folk like them I knew. I said they'd probably drink in turn from the jug. That's if we gave 'em what they wanted. They were standing at the gate now, all smoking. They leaned their heads in and lit three cigs from one match. No, I tell a lie: two cigs, 'cos three's bad luck. Two, and the third was lit off the end of one of the others.

' "I don't want everybody thinking they can knock on the door and demand a jug of tea."

' "I'll tell 'em not to tell anybody."

'So she asks me if there's any left in the can, and when I say yes, she says to pour it into an enamel jug. Nothing about warming it up, but I think I can do that without asking once her back's turned.

' "And shall I give it to 'em?" I'm asking and she says with her lips pursed, "You will not. You'll ask 'em for tuppence. We've all got to live, y'know."

'Though I've always wondered why some folk think they've more right to live than others.

'He came back towards the end of the week after. I know it wasn't the same day because one or two things were different: the missus had gone to market for one thing, so there wasn't her to be pursing her lips. He'd have been back sooner if he'd lived nearer; I knew that from the way he looked at me: no mistaking his interest, but still with that little touch of shyness in it. "Want a photograph?" I asked him. That made him start. "You what?" "Staring," I said. "Lookin's free, i'n't it?" he said, and I said, "Not always." And, of course, it wasn't for him. Lookin' at me cost him his freedom. He looked and saw summat what drew him, and between-times he must have had me in his mind like I had him, because he came back. On his own.

' "No mates this time?"

'He shakes his head, his eyes never leaving my face. "No."

' "Fed up with the joys of country life, are they, or have they found work to go to?"

'Well, of course, they hadn't found work and they were a while before any of them did, which was what held us up when we decided to get wed.

'I guessed that his mates didn't even know he'd come again. What he'd come back for was private and he didn't want them around to watch or try to put him off.

' "How long does it take you?" I asked him.

' "An hour."

' "There must be sights just as bonny nearer home." '

' "No." He shakes his head again.

'It was a warm morning. The sun had got out early.

' "Will you be wanting some tea again?"

' "If it's no trouble."

'I told him to come round and led him to the kitchen door. He wouldn't cross the threshold till I pressed him and told him the master and the missus were away at market.

' "Sit down," I told him. "Eat your bait. What do you call it – your snap? Eat your snap. Have you got summat tasty?"

' "Jam an' bread."

' "Oh, I like a slice o' pork dripping, meself."

' "So do I, when there is some. But jam an' bread's better down t'pit. It works some spit up, to cut the dust."

' "Is it home-made?"

' "Oh aye. Raspberry. Want a taste?"

' "No, thanks. I had me breakfast not all that long since.

' "You don't get up till t'best part o' t'day's over."

' "We work *before* breakfast here. I wor up at six."

' "It's all right me being in here, then, is it?" he asks, switching the subject without a sorry.

' "Yes. Eat your snap. There's nobody to bother you."

'I was wrong there, as it turned out. I'd forgotten that the gaffer had left Mole Templeton working in the home field, and Mole, having a bit of a fancy for me – whether it was for me meself or just for getting me on me own in the stackyard, I never rightly knew – he come round when he thought the coast was clear and finds me entertainin' a stranger eating jam an' bread and drinking tea in the missus's kitchen.

' "Drop o' that left for a thirsty worker?" Mole asks, and nods at the pot on the table. "I could sup a well dry today." He's brought his bottle with him as an excuse, and I say I'll fill it for him to take back with him.

'All the time Mole's standing in the open doorway,

looking Thomas over, weighing him up, judging his build and his likely handiness with his fists an' all, if I know him. Sort of dark and tight and muscle-y, Mole. Nowt to spare on him.

' "Come far?" he says in the end.

' " 'Bout twenty mile."

' "Tidy step. Down on your luck?"

' "I'm not workin', if that's what you mean."

' "There's nowt round here," Mole says. "I know that for a fact."

' "I'm not lookin'."

' "A long way to come for nothin'."

'He's quizzin', Mole is, dying to know; and Thomas doesn't enlighten him. And then it's just as though something inside me says "the hell with it", because I hear meself speaking out and surprising everybody.

' "He's come to see me."

'I can see I've startled Thomas by the way he puts his pot down and goes very still. And Mole . . . well, Mole doesn't rightly know what to do, because his chances of gettin' his hands on me have vanished in that couple of seconds.

' "I hope," he says then, "that the missus doesn't get to know 'at you do your courting in her kitchen while her back's turned."

' "You hope she doesn't get to know," I say, "but you'll make it in your way to tell her."

' "If you're going to be like that."

'I hold out his bottle. "Here's your tea."

' "What did you say that for?" Thomas says when Mole's gone.

' "What?"

' " 'At I'd come to see you."

' "I thought you had."

'He looks round the kitchen and says, "There's not a lot o' future in this, though, is there?"

' "It'll do to be goin' on with."

' "Is there no chance of seeing you away from here?"

' "I don't know."

' "They don't work you twenty-four hours a day, do they?"

' "It sometimes feels like it."

' "D'you live in?"

'I told him I did: that the farm had been home for me ever since me dad died and the landlord wanted his house for somebody else.

' "You're all on your own in t'world, are you?"

'I told him yes.

' "So if yon' chap makes trouble for you, you could likely end up wi' no roof over your head as well as no job? Eh?"

'That was when I asked him about his family and heard about you lot. Being one of a big family, Ella, and t'youngest an' all, I don't suppose you can imagine what it's like for somebody looking in from outside: somebody on their own 'at's never known what it is to have a brother or a sister. It seems like you could never be lonely, never without somebody to stick up for you. Thomas never painted a picture like that, mind: I did that for meself, and the way I'd been feeling while I was dependent on them at the farm, nobody could have stopped me doing it.

'So I made me mind up 'at I was going to have him; and as it wasn't in me nature to lead a chap on and play hard to get, I decided I'd let him have anything he wanted. I don't know how much you gave in to Walter before you were wed, and I'm not asking you to tell me. That's your business. But I gave in to Thomas. I gave in every time I saw him and we could find somewhere private – in a wood, a corner of a field, an old shed. I'd have taken him into me bed but the house was never empty long enough – or when it was, there was always somebody on the doorstep. But we managed. Yes, he was a lusty man, Thomas. He had big appetites. That was one I thought I could satisfy. I did me best, anyway; and I knew full well the risk I was taking. I don't just mean getting pregnant. I mean that he'd come for that and that

186

alone, and do a bunk the minute anything more permanent was mentioned.

'You know the rest. As much as you need to know. As much as I can tell you, any road. How old were you when we got married? Old enough to know. God help us! we weren't married ten minutes. We had our fifth anniversary only last month. And now it's all over.

'But what I've told you's a love story. It is, isn't it, Ella?'

# Fifteen

You could live in a smallish place all your life and there
still be parts of it where you'd never been: yards
and streets tucked away off the thoroughfares you
habitually used.

Ella stood looking round. Street names had been
removed along with signposts earlier that summer.

'Are you lost?'

An old man had come to the door of his terrace house.
Despite the warm weather he wore a cardigan over his
waistcoat and a woollen jumper between waistcoat and
shirt.

'It looks like it.'

'Where was it you were looking for?'

'Purcell Street.'

'You're near. You're not a German parachutist, by the
way, are you?'

'Do I look like one?'

'Nay, I don't know. I've never seen one. Not to me
knowledge, anyway.'

'I'm looking for somebody called Sims, number seven
Purcell Street.'

'It's that street across t'top, up there.'

'Ta.'

'Mrs Sims is out, though, I believe. I'm nearly sure I
saw her pass here half an hour ago.'

'That's all right. I work with their Olive.'

'Oh.' The old man nodded. He looked as if he would
have liked to talk a little longer, but Ella gave him a
'Ta-ra' and walked on.

Olive had said her mother was going out. That was why she had asked Ella round, so that they could have a good talk without anyone else looking and listening.

'What's it all about, though?' Ella had asked.

'What d'you think it's about?'

'Is it summat to do with you and Tony?'

She might have jumped to the obvious conclusion that Olive had got pregnant, except that there was no hint of panic in her demeanour.

'Yes. I want your advice. Will you come?'

'All right.'

She had changed her library books on the way, and carried the replacements in an oilcloth bag. Purcell Street was an unmade street of half a dozen houses a side, a cul-de-sac which ended in a low stone wall with a fringe of trees, then a meadow where cattle grazed. Doors stood open in the soft evening air, and from one interior came the sounds of a child being chastised. Surprisingly, though, at the moment, there were no children playing out and no one sitting in doorways to watch her as she walked along.

Olive was wearing a white blouse, a pleated tartan skirt and a funny little smile when she answered Ella's knock. 'Come in.' Ella stepped into the little square lobby at the foot of the stairs. The in-door was shut. She could smell Olive's scent now: some sort of flower fragrance that she didn't care for and which Olive had applied with a liberal hand.

'Me mam's gone,' Olive said; yet already then Ella had this sudden feeling that they were not alone, before Olive opened the door and ushered her into the living-room.

Both men were already on their feet, seeming to fill the room with towering khaki; and as silly Olive said, 'Look who's here,' Ella was struck dumb, her heart pumping with the surprise of seeing them and the knowledge that she had been tricked.

Tony said, 'Hi, Ella. How're you doing?'

Ella swallowed. 'How'm I doing?' Her voice sounded

189

throaty, strangled. 'I was doing all right, but I don't know now. I've been led up the garden path.'

She saw something flit across Howard's face.

'Didn't you know we'd be here? Olive said you'd agreed to come.'

'Olive might not mind havin' t'neighbours see her entertaining soldiers while her mother's out, but she's gone a bit far when she –'

'Me mam knows about Tony,' Olive said. Her mother was a widow and, far from being the rather starchy and censorious woman Ella had imagined, apparently had boy friends of her own. Things like that Ella had learned since she had been drawn closer to Olive.

'That's your business,' Ella said, 'but when you drag me into it you make it mine an' all. I'm just glad,' she said to Howard, ' 'at you apparently weren't a party to it.' She turned and went to the in-door. 'If I go now there'll happen be no harm done. I'll see you at work, Olive. We'll sort it out then.'

'Ella.' Olive had taken her by the arm. 'They're leavin'. They're goin' away.'

'When?'

'Tomorrow. It's t'only reason I deceived you. You wouldn't ha' come, otherwise.'

'*Wouldn't* you have come?' Howard asked.

Ella shrugged. Her anger had subsided into surliness. 'I don't know.' She didn't.

'Well, now you're here you can stay for a minute,' Tony said. 'Surely.'

'You were in on it, were you?' Ella asked.

'Yes, I was. Who would you have thanked if we'd left without you knowing?'

'I don't know what you think it's got to do with me,' Ella burst out. 'It's none o' my business. I was living here before you came an' I'll be living here when you've gone.'

There was a sofa with two easy chairs grouped round the fireplace. The table leaves let down to make room for them. Olive led Ella back into the room. 'Sit yourself

190

down and don't get your hair off.' Ella sat on the edge of a seat.

'I was sorry to hear about your brother,' Howard said.

'How did you know about that?'

'Everybody knew about the disaster. Olive told us you had somebody involved.'

'Where are they sending you to?' she asked abruptly.

'We don't know.'

'Some say India, some say Iceland,' Tony said.

Olive began to cry. It was like a tap being turned on. 'This bloody war.'

'We wouldn't have met without it,' Tony pointed out.

'I know.' She was twisting her hankie in her lap. Tony sat down beside her and put his arm round her shoulders.

'I'll write, you know. Don't worry about that.'

'You can't cuddle flamin' letters,' Olive said.

It occurred to Ella that her presence was spoiling an ideal opportunity for them to cuddle to their hearts' content. She began to rise.

'I'm just in your way.'

'Me too, if it comes to that,' Howard said.

'Where are you going?' Olive said. 'You can't walk the streets together.' She put her mouth to Tony's ear and spoke in a rapid whisper.

'If you say so,' he said.

Olive got up. She didn't look at Ella. 'You can have this room.' She went out. Her feet pounded on the lino-covered stairs as Tony crossed the room after her.

'I'll give three knocks on the top step when we're coming back,' he said. He went upstairs lightfooted, with hardly a sound.

'What's he mean, "three knocks"?' Ella said. 'What does he think we're goin' to be doing?'

Howard shrugged. 'Oh, he's like that.'

Ella looked up at the ceiling. 'Does he care tuppence about her?'

'They seem to get on.'

'How long will he remember her once she's out of sight?'

'I don't know,' Howard said. 'And we're doing it again, aren't we?'

'What?'

'Talking about *them*.'

'What else is there to talk about?'

'You've got a callous streak I'd never have suspected.'

'I call it common sense.'

'Will you let me write to *you*?'

'I don't like to refuse you; but what for? And how?'

'I can write care of Olive.'

'Well, I can't stop you. But don't expect me to reply.'

'You've really set your face against me, haven't you?'

'I'm a married woman, Howard.' She said it slowly and clearly, as if repeating a lesson he would not take in.

'Does that mean you've got nothing against me personally?'

'Why should I have? You've never done nothing to me.'

'I mean you don't dislike me.'

'You know I don't. What more do you want me to say?'

'I want to know that you'll remember me when I'm gone.'

'I remembered you before. Why shouldn't I now?'

'Because I think you'd already decided to shut me right out of your mind.'

'Thinking it's one thing; doing it's another.'

'Is it, Ella? Is it really?'

His voice was suddenly eager. She had not meant to encourage him, but he was ready to clutch at any tiny advantage she gave him. He shifted along the sofa to the end nearest her and reached across the gap to take her hand.

'No gloves tonight.'

'No.'

'Nothing to hide any more?'

'I wear 'em when I'm dressed up.'

'And you didn't know this evening was anything special, did you?'

'They're not hands for showing off anyway,' Ella said.

'They do too much work.' When he did not speak she said, unable to resist the jibe, 'You've got gentleman's hands. You and Mr Keighley. I noticed when you first came.' When she was still single; before he was convicted as a thief; before there was a war. Before everything had changed so irrevocably.

He held out his free hand, still holding hers with the other.

'I don't take any special care of them.'

'No, but they're not allus in grease and muck, are they? I couldn't keep nails like that for five minutes.'

Quietly, he turned her hand over and, letting it rest in his, began tracing circles in her palm with his thumb. She withdrew it as though it had touched something hot.

'What d'you think you're doing?'

'What *am* I doing?' He seemed genuinely puzzled.

'Don't you know what that means?'

'What?'

'When you tickle a lass's palm?'

'No. Is it something . . .?'

'Yes, it is.' But she felt slightly foolish now in the speed of her reaction: silly, adolescent.

'I'm sorry. I don't think I've heard of that before. Do you suppose it's what Olive did to Tony before they went upstairs?'

He was making fun of her. She said before she realised it, 'I've a feeling they don't need that any more.'

'She's your friend. You should know.'

'Tony's your friend.'

'But men boast. What they say can't always be trusted.'

'He hasn't been boasting about Olive, has he?'

'Not a word out of place.'

Ella thought she heard the splutter of a woman's laughter from upstairs. There was a thud, as though something had fallen. Surprising herself, she realised that she was chuckling.

'That's more like it,' Howard said. 'Though you might share the joke.'

Ella jerked her head at the ceiling. 'I'm thinking about that chap what daren't drop off to sleep till he's heard the second boot fall.'

'So long as we can enjoy a laugh,' Howard said, 'there's still hope.'

He was looking at her now, with that look she could not return, taking all in as if to burn every detail deep into his memory.

'Stop it,' she said, when she couldn't stand it any longer.

'What?'

'*Staring.*'

'I can't help it. And there's not much time left.'

'What time will you go?'

'We parade straight after breakfast.'

'Will they move you in lorries, or what?'

'Special train.'

'You'll be marching to the station, then.'

'Yes. In full kit. Will you be there to watch?'

'I can't break me work.'

'We'd better say goodbye now, then?'

'I suppose so.'

He sat slightly forwards, his hands hanging between his knees. Ella examined the folded rim of her bag, noting how it was stitched.

Finally, she said, '*Will* you write?'

'Do you want me to?'

She swallowed, hung her head. He had to say again, 'Do you want me to?'

'I don't think . . .' she began; 'I didn't ought to say so, but I don't think I could bear it if you were just lost and I didn't know where. There's surely no harm in that,' she added in a moment.

'None at all,' Howard said.

He leaned further forward as both his hands reached to take hers. The bag slid off her lap and on to the hearthrug as she let herself be drawn towards him. He moved to make a space for her between himself and the arm of the sofa and she sank into it and was taken close

194

by his encircling arm. Her face was against his shoulder. His free hand touched her hair, then traced the line of her flushed cheek. Her body trembled with a long shuddering sigh. She could not stop it: not *this*, anyway. And it was enough. There were other things she dared not let her thoughts dwell on. For now – for all time as far as he was concerned – she must be content, as indeed she was, to lie against him and float in a waking dream in which yearning and fulfilment seemed to fuse in a single feeling. Time passed. There was no sound now from upstairs. Once, she started as next door's wireless suddenly blared with foghorn voices, but when he soothed her with little gentle movements she relaxed against him once more with the incoherent murmur of a child momentarily disturbed in sleep. Neither of them spoke, not even when, after no one knew how long, he turned her face so that he could kiss her and she felt her lips open and soften to his. Vaguely, at the far edge of her awareness, was the knowledge that they could at any moment be disturbed, and that what seemed to her so inevitable, so right, could be misconstrued, mocked, reviled and held up as a reason for shame.

But no one came.

Through an oval looking-glass on the inner wall she could see the sky above the lace-curtained lower half of the sash-window. It was still light, though all the brightness had gone. It was still light when most people had gone to bed. The sound of the wireless next door had long ago settled to an indistinct rumble. There had been for a little while the voices of children being allowed to tire themselves in the street before they were sent to try to sleep in airless and only partly darkened bedrooms. But this now had gone, somehow just ceased while her attention was not on it. She did not know when Howard and Tony might be due back in barracks, but she was in touch with the reality of the world beyond the window enough to realise that she should find out what time it was now while the kind of excuses she could invent to explain her long absence would still serve. But when he stirred, turning his face to hers, and spoke for the first time since taking her to him, saying 'Ella. Ella, my love,' she put all else from her mind except the offering again of soft willing lips.

Some time later, on her feet in the room now crowded with Olive and Tony and a woman wearing far too much scarlet lipstick and scent, who Olive said was her mother though she did not resemble her in the least, Ella swayed as if she had been wrested from a deep sleep and thrust immediately upright.

Mrs Sims expressed surprise that Olive had not offered her friends a cup of anything, and left a smell of beer in Ella's nostrils as she brushed by and went into the scullery to put a kettle on.

'I've got to go,' Ella said.

Olive gave her a look that was almost a leer, and asked if Ella was glad she had come now.

Ella stepped closer to her. 'Look, Olive, can you explain to your mam somehow? Tell her to –'

'Oh, don't worry. Me mam can keep her mouth shut. Live an' let live is what she always says.'

Ella spoke to Tony: 'Well, be good, and if you can't be good be careful.'

Howard, as she had known he would, followed her into the lobby. There he took her and pressed her to him full length from mouth to knees, all dreamy languor gone in the desperation of imminent parting.

'What can we do, Ella? What can we do?'

'Apart from you looking out for yourself – nothing. Write and let me know how you are.'

He would have held her again but she opened the street-door and stepped out.

'I've forgotten me bag.'

He went for it. She took it from him, nodded, and walked away.

The streets seemed as deserted as they were in the dawn walk to the mill, and she had the curious impression that the light was poised in its fading, arrested, as though it might reverse into full day again. How *had* all that time passed by? She had no key, so her father would probably be waiting up for her. 'We got talking,' she could hear herself saying. 'You don't realise how time's flown.'

He had been very quiet, her father, since Thomas's death. All in his personality of lively inquiry had gone or become subdued. He brooded, saying little. She hoped he would be waiting and not her mother. The last thing she wanted tonight was to talk to anybody. If she had a hot drink alone and got to bed, she might before she slept make some sense of her thoughts. She didn't think so, but she could try.

She walked on. The buses had stopped running; the pub doors were firmly shut. There were not even any drunks about, singing or arguing the toss. A black cat walked along a wall over her head. It stopped and arched its back. Across an intersection a uniformed policeman stepped out on to the pavement after trying the door of the Co-op Chemists. He lifted his hand when she nodded to him, and stood to watch her go.

'Surely,' she thought, 'I'm not the only person out. It can't be *that* late.'

No, she was not. Firm footsteps could be heard on her left. They came nearer. She had passed the ginnel, and glanced back as the man emerged from it. He was in uniform and he lifted his hand high as he saw her, and trotted towards her across the road.

'Ella, where've you been till this time? I've looked all over for you. Where've you been?'

Ella thought she might faint. It was Walter.

# Sixteen

How the heck, Ella wanted to know – turning the questions from herself – had he managed to travel all that way without her knowing he was coming?

He had beaten his letter. When he posted it he hadn't known that he would be one of those they found room for in a transport aircraft returning immediately to Britain. But then, he had thought with glee all the way home, via Newfoundland and Iceland, what a wonderful surprise it would be for her.

'So you might look as if you're glad to see me.'

'I might if I could get me breath back. Surprise you call it. For all I know you're five thousand miles away, when you come walking out of Workhouse Ginnel and give me the shock of me life.'

Sugden and Patience seemed under the impression that he had finished his training and might be up in the air again tomorrow. They would have believed him if he'd told them he had flown the aeroplane across the Atlantic himself. But Ella knew different. They had both waited up while he roamed the streets looking for her, too impatient to let her come home in her own good time. Now they went to bed, later than usual, but happy in the knowledge that Walter had come so far, at least, apparently unscathed.

Then Ella did not know how to ask him without the risk of wounding his vanity. She waited until he had her on her feet and held against him, his hands pressing her breasts. His hunger for her was shameless. He could not leave her alone. He sat down in the rocker and pulled her on to his knee, his hand sliding under her skirt to fondle the inside of her bare leg. She pinned it there, stopping it from going further.

'Steady on, Walter.'

'Be right, Ella! I've thought about nowt else all the way across the Atlantic.'

'You can surely wait a bit longer, then?'

'All right, all right.' She could feel him hard under her thigh and wondered that she didn't hurt him. He nuzzled his mouth into her ear. 'You're as ready as I am, if the truth be told. Aren't you? I know you are.'

Her hope was that she could keep him believing it.

'Why have they sent you home?'

'Why do you think?'

'I suppose it must be such tickle work they can only pass the very, very best.'

'Oh, you take it for granted they've chucked me out. You don't think I could have done the work in a third of the time.'

'I'm not saying you didn't do your best. At least you got taken for training; some people never get that far.'

'Better if I hadn't,' he said. 'It's worse to be given the chance and then blow it.'

'It's nowt to be ashamed of Walter, honest. Don't take it so much to heart. There'll be summat else you can do.'

'I can dress a carcase,' he said. 'I ought to have gone into the flippin' Catering Corps, where I belong.'

'You're bound to feel bad about it now, but you'll get over it in time. I don't suppose you were the only one, were you?'

'Oh, no. But I don't like being in the rejects squad.'

'I don't mind telling you that I shall feel a sight easier knowing you're on the ground.'

'If every wife thought like you, Ella, there'd be nobody to fight at all.'

'Them that's in the air need reliable people on the ground. Isn't that right?'

'Oh, aye.'

'So you just get to be as good as you can at whatever it is they make you do next.'

'It's all I can do.'

'No, it isn't. You could get bitter and sorry for yourself and never do anything right again.'

'You know me better than that.'

'I hope I do.'

'You won't go round telling folk why I'm back so soon, though, will you?'

'You know me better than that.'

'Aye. Have you missed me, then?'

'Aye.'

'I tried to tell you what I felt, in my letters.'

'I noticed.'

'It's funny. I'd never have thought I was much of a letter-writer, but somehow I found I could say things then easier than I can to your face.'

'Hmmm . . .'

'What's up now?'

'Me leg's gone to sleep.'

'Oh, all right then . . .'

'Have you had any supper?'

'I had some fish and chips while I was out.'

'We'd better get to bed, then. I've to be up at six.'

'Six nowt,' Walter said. 'I'm not spending my first morning on leave waving you off to work. You can laik a shift. Mebbe two or three, but that one to start with. When I get you to bed I want you to stop there for a while.'

Free of her weight, he stretched and yawned, then took out cigarettes and a big shiny lighter with a top that flipped open.

'Have you started smoking again?'

'Everybody smokes,' Walter said. 'Chaps 'at fly, they smoke like chimneys and drink like fish.' They were cigarettes in a soft paper packet of a kind Ella had not seen before. 'I'd got to rather fancy the idea of a pipe.'

'Why don't you?'

'Not now, love. That went with the wings.'

'Is there anything special you want to do while you're here?'

'Roll over at reveille time for a start. Then have me breakfast any time I feel like it. By, but the grub they have over there, Ella! Steaks that lap over the edge of your plate; great rashers of ham that thick –'

'It's to be hoped you've brought some food coupons with you,' Ella said, ' 'cos we're down to four ounces of bacon a week. We've even got tea rationing now. Two ounces. I don't know what good they think it'll do the war effort when people can't have a decent cup of tea. It's enough to drive us all to drink.'

' "Take me back to dear old Blighty",' Walter said. He got up and embraced her again. 'There's some things that aren't rationed, though, eh? And I'll tell you summat: it's one thing that's the same for rich and poor alike. There's some o' t'better off 'at don't like that, but it is so.' He fondled her bottom and gave her a light kiss. 'Have you done all your jobs?'

'Yes.'

'Off you go up, then. I've just to pop out to the back, then I'll join you. By the way,' he said as she turned to go, 'is your best nightie ironed?'

'My honeymoon nightie's clean.'

'Good-oh! Just make sure you pop it safe under your pillow, where you can find it if there's a fire.'

'Walter!'


He was enormous in her hands. With his mouth at her nipple she felt the sluggish stir of a pleasure that might awaken enough to save his leave. But not now. Now she must play for time . . .

'Walter . . .'

'Mmm . . .?'

'Just for tonight, will you . . .?'

'What's wrong?'

'It's nothing, but down there I'm a bit, well, sore.'

'Sore?'

201

'More itchy-like.'

'What is it?'

'It's nothing serious. It comes every now and again, then goes when I bathe it.'

'What have you been doing?'

'Nothing. It's what you eat and drink. The time of year. Mebbe being without you, after we'd been together so much.'

'Well, I can soon remedy that.'

'I know, but not tonight, eh?'

'Oh, hell, Ella . . .'

'I don't know if it's something I could pass on to you, either.'

'Bloody hell! They show us horror films about things like that.'

'It's not anything like that. How can it be? I'm sure it'll be all right by tomorrow. Be patient and I'll make it up to you.'

'God, I can't remember when I was so randy.'

'Let me finish you this way, then. That's nice as well, isn't it?'

'Mmm . . .'

'Ooh, but you know, you feel half as big again as you were before you went away.'

'Oh, you know how it is,' Walter said; 'everything's king-size in Canada.'

At which they both began to giggle and splutter in the dark, the bed shaking and creaking under them.

Ella dug him in the ribs. 'Shurrup, will you, you big gorby. Me mam an' dad 'ull be thinking . . .'

'What?'

'You know what.'

'Well, come on, then.'

'No, Walter, I've told you.'

'Well, put your hands back where they belong. There . . . that one there. Like that . . . Don't be rough . . . Take it gently . . . Oh, yes, Ella, that's lovely . . .'

His voice died, leaving the hot gust of his breath in the

bend of her neck and shoulder. His upper hand clutched and kneaded her breast until she felt the pump of his climax, when it relaxed and fell away as his body slackened beside her and subsided into a dead weight. She had the impression that he had fallen asleep on the instant. No reason, she thought, why he shouldn't. There was nothing to haunt him. He was where he had every right to be, his wife's bed, with all that he could expect of that. Peace, peace, peace, in one short interval of war.

In a concern for the sheet and what it would look like brought to wash, she had at the last cupped her hand. Now as she felt the thick abundant slickness on her skin, the fancy came to her that she held in her palm enough life to replace them all: Ronald, Edward, David, Wilson, Ada, John, Doris, Thomas, herself. In a moment she turned on to her back and, opening her hand, pressed it against her and drew it between her breasts to her navel. Then, vaguely surprised at the intensity of its coming, she gave herself up to sleep.

She woke in the morning at the usual time, a minute or two before her father gave her her knock. When she heard him, instead of calling she slipped out of bed and crossed the room, remembering before she reached the door that she was naked. She opened the door an inch and spoke through the gap.

'I'm having a shift, Dad. Walter doesn't want me to go. I'm sorry I couldn't tell you last night.'

'It's all right. I was waken anyway.'

Walter was turned away from her and still sleeping soundly, his breathing steady. She got into bed again and curled up against his back, telling herself that she would go downstairs and make some tea if she didn't fall asleep inside the next ten minutes or so.

The next time she woke it was to the sound of marching feet in the road outside. The sun had moved round as far as this window, and it bathed Walter as he crouched to see out. He glanced round at her as he heard the mattress creak.

203

'Ella, it's the soldiers. They're marching away.'

'Oh, *that* station,' Ella said before she could think.

'You what?'

'The station. That's where they'll be going.'

For some reason she had imagined the station on the opposite side of the town, never thinking that they might march right past the house.

'Aren't you coming to look?' When she didn't answer, he said, 'I never knew there were so many of 'em. I wonder where they're bound for.'

'I don't suppose they know themselves.'

'They have all their kit with them.'

'Good luck to them.'

'Aren't you coming to look?' he asked again.

'I can't be bothered.'

She watched him as the boots tramped by. He had not covered himself and she was astonishingly, acutely aware of the rightness, the authority, of his body as he crouched, naked, at the window: the rounded tips of his shoulders, the muscles moving in his back; the tight moons of his behind below the lean waist; and, below the flat belly, visible as he half-turned to glance as if to make sure she was still there, the slack, heavy sag of cock and balls in the clump of hair that the sunlight tinted fiery gold, as though it held a haze of pollen.

'I wonder,' he said, 'how many broken hearts this lot are leaving behind.'

'How many did you leave behind?' Ella asked.

'A hundred and thirty-two,' he answered promptly.

He caught her smile as he looked across at her. She was sitting up against the pillows now, the quilt tucked under her armpits.

He said, 'Have I to come back in for a while?'

'If you like.'

'Did you see 'em?' Patience asked when Ella went down.

'Walter did. I just heard 'em.'

Her mother and father had been out to watch.

204

'A funny thing . . .' Patience began.

She poured tea. The house-door stood open. It promised to be another glorious day.

'What's funny?' Ella asked.

'Watching all them young men just now. Your father doesn't believe me.'

'You were dreaming,' Sugden said.

'What doesn't he believe?'

'I could have sworn,' Patience said, 'that one of 'em was the living spit of that Mr Strickland.'

Walter had come into the room from the stairs, braces dangling, his manner easy, comfortable, at home.

'Who's Mr Strickland?' Ella heard him ask as she went through the door into the yard.

There was already heat in the day. With new-laid eggs in her hands, she re-fastened the chicken-wire gate of the hen-run and stood in a stillness which strutting poultry seemed only to emphasise. Nor did she move when a train whistled in the cutting, three-quarters of a mile away. She felt she had been carried along by events ever since entering Olive's house, and now, at last, she had a minute to herself. She felt that she was standing at the still centre of a colossal turmoil; and for someone so small and insignificant that could only mean that she had drawn from somewhere the power to create that stillness in herself. She was fearful of examining it too closely; who knew that if it vanished she would ever assemble its ingredients again? But she was struck by an impression now of being watched by her younger self; a girl with a ribbon in her hair and a yearning for something and somewhere else, for someone else who would embody all their grace and charm; a girl she had said good-bye to last night in Purcell Street.

In a minute or two, she was sure, Walter would come out to look for her, and she wanted to be ready when he asked again, as he always asked a question again until he got an answer he could understand: 'Who's Mr Strickland?' Because she intended to tell him everything

205

he needed to know, in one short sentence, spoken with all the truth she could muster: 'Nobody you need bother about.'

She heard a voice.

'Day-dreaming?' Mildred Sadler-Browne was looking over the wall. 'You were miles away.'

Ella's private little smile as she shook her head made Mrs Sadler-Browne narrow her eyes.

'No, I wasn't,' she said. 'I was right here.'

THE END

# A Kind of Loving
## Stan Barstow

As probably the best example of work produced by British
novelists in the 1960s, A KIND OF LOVING is now
regarded as a classic of post-war literature.

Immortalised first as a film and then as a highly-acclaimed
television series, Stan Barstow's novel is as alive and as
relevant today as when its author was described on first
publication as having 'warmth, liveliness, honesty and
compassion'
SUNDAY TIMES

The first of a trilogy (THE WATCHERS ON THE SHORE
and THE RIGHT TRUE END are both published in Black
Swan). A KIND OF LOVING tells how young Vic Brown
comes to terms – the hard way – with adult life and his
feelings for the beautiful but demanding Ingrid.

0 552 99186 4

# BLACK SWAN

# A SELECTED LIST OF
# OTHER BLACK SWAN TITLES

THE PRICES SHOWN BELOW WERE CORRECT AT THE TIME OF GOING TO PRESS.
HOWEVER TRANSWORLD PUBLISHERS RESERVE THE RIGHT TO SHOW NEW RETAIL
PRICES ON COVERS WHICH MAY DIFFER FROM THOSE PREVIOUSLY ADVERTISED IN
THE TEXT OR ELSEWHERE.

| | | | |
|---|---|---|---|
| ☐ 99198 8 | THE HOUSE OF THE SPIRITS | Isabel Allende | £4.99 |
| ☐ 99313 1 | OF LOVE AND SHADOWS | Isabel Allende | £3.95 |
| ☐ 99248 8 | THE DONE THING | Patricia Angadi | £4.95 |
| ☐ 99201 1 | THE GOVERNESS | Patricia Angadi | £3.95 |
| ☐ 99185 6 | THE DESPERADOES | Stan Barstow | £3.95 |
| ☐ 99193 7 | A RAGING CALM | Stan Barstow | £4.95 |
| ☐ 99186 4 | A KIND OF LOVING | Stan Barstow | £3.99 |
| ☐ 99189 9 | WATCHERS ON THE SHORE | Stan Barstow | £3.95 |
| ☐ 99187 2 | THE RIGHT TRUE END | Stan Barstow | £3.99 |
| ☐ 99321 2 | B MOVIE | Stan Barstow | £3.95 |
| ☐ 99159 7 | THE GLAD EYE AND OTHER STORIES | Stan Barstow | £3.50 |
| ☐ 99176 7 | JOBY | Stan Barstow | £2.95 |
| ☐ 99075 2 | QUEEN LUCIA | E.F. Benson | £3.95 |
| ☐ 99076 0 | LUCIA IN LONDON | E.F. Benson | £3.99 |
| ☐ 99083 3 | MISS MAPP | E.F. Benson | £3.95 |
| ☐ 99084 1 | MAPP AND LUCIA | E.F. Benson | £3.95 |
| ☐ 99087 6 | LUCIA'S PROGRESS | E.F. Benson | £3.95 |
| ☐ 99088 4 | TROUBLE FOR LUCIA | E.F. Benson | £3.95 |
| ☐ 99202 X | LUCIA IN WARTIME | Tom Holt | £3.50 |
| ☐ 99281 X | LUCIA TRIUMPHANT | Tom Holt | £3.99 |
| ☐ 99228 3 | A FINE EXCESS | Jane Ellison | £3.95 |
| ☐ 99257 7 | THE KILLJOY | Anne Fine | £3.95 |
| ☐ 99130 9 | NOAH'S ARK | Barbara Trapido | £2.95 |
| ☐ 99056 6 | BROTHER OF THE MORE FAMOUS JACK | Barbara Trapido | £3.95 |
| ☐ 99117 1 | MRS POOTER'S DIARY | Keith Waterhouse | £3.95 |
| ☐ 99210 0 | HARNESSING PEACOCKS | Mary Wesley | £3.99 |
| ☐ 99126 0 | THE CAMOMILE LAWN | Mary Wesley | £3.99 |
| ☐ 99082 5 | JUMPING THE QUEUE | Mary Wesley | £3.50 |
| ☐ 99258 5 | THE VACILLATIONS OF POPPY CAREW | Mary Wesley | £3.99 |
| ☐ 99304 2 | NOT THAT SORT OF GIRL | Mary Wesley | £3.99 |

*All Black Swan Books are available at your bookshop or newsagent, or can be ordered from the
following address:*

Corgi/Bantam Books,
Cash Sales Department,
P.O. Box 11, Falmouth, Cornwall TR10 9EN

Please send a cheque or postal order (no currency) and allow 60p for postage and packing for
the first book plus 25p for the second book and 15p for each additional book ordered up to a
maximum charge of £1.90 in UK.

B.F.P.O. customers please allow 60p for the first book, 25p for the second book plus 15p per
copy for the next 7 books, thereafter 9p per book.

Overseas customers, including Eire, please allow £1.25 for postage and packing for the first
book, 75p for the second book, and 28p for each subsequent title ordered.